The
ROCKING
HORSE

GLORIA ZACHGO

ACKNOWLEDGMENTS

I first want to thank all of my writing friends for their encouragement and advice, especially Mary Johnson. She opened up a new world to me through writing and made me realize that it could take me anywhere my imagination wanted to go.

Thank you to my husband, Ron, for his patience. He kept me positive enough to pursue my dreams and share my book with others.

And last, but certainly not least, thank you to my good friend, Marion Duer, for listening, reading, suggesting, editing, and most of all giving me the confidence to continue through until the end of this journey.

SHADY CREEK, KANSAS
Twenty-two Years Ago

~ 1 ~

Amanda Preston didn't notice the car that was slowly following her and her two-year-old daughter, Jenny, as they walked down the quiet street. A brewing rainstorm teased the ground with its first drops of refreshing wetness on the hot sidewalk. It was a smell so sweet that Amanda wished she could bottle it and use it whenever she needed a smile. Scooping Jenny up in her arms, both giggled as Amanda began to run. They reached the back door of Aunt Ruth and Uncle Don's new house just as the cloudburst let loose.

Amanda gave a quick rap on the door to announce their arrival, "Knock, knock, anybody home?" They went through the unlocked door into Aunt Ruthie's kitchen. Hardly anyone in Shady Creek bothered to lock their doors.

"Hi girls. Jenny, what a nice surprise to see you!" Ruth Shepman glowed as Amanda and the child rushed in.

Jenny ran over to her great aunt's wheelchair and gave her knees a hug. "Cook—cook." she managed to say as she proudly held up a slightly crushed gingerbread man to her aunt.

"A cookie? For me?" laughed Ruth. "Ooh, my favorite!" Feigning surprise and delight she took the gingerbread man from Jenny. Holding it up to her nose and inhaling deeply, she said, "It smells luscious!"

"Jenny and Mom made them for you this afternoon while I was at work. Jenny thought you needed to have a cookie party in your new home," explained Amanda.

"Thank you so much, Jenny," Ruth smiled. "Do you think we should gobble this gingerbread man up?"

Jenny's reddish blond curls bounced as her head bobbed. Gingerbread cookies were her favorite too. Amanda was already getting glasses and napkins out for the feast. She opened the container that held more cookies and was pouring milk when her Uncle Don and his friend Jimmy popped into the room.

"Hi, Uncle Don," Amanda said. She walked over to him and gave him a quick hug. "Hi, Jimmy."

"Hi," came a shy reply from Jimmy.

Jimmy Barclay was often at the Shepman house. Jimmy was a twenty-seven-year-old man who had the reasoning power of a nine-year-old boy. His body grew fast and large, but his mental capacity simply did not develop with the rest of him. He stood just over six feet and had the physical strength of a man. His nature was gentle, yet he appeared strange to some of the townspeople. When they saw such a big guy act like the child his mind restricted him to be, prejudices and superstitions arose. And though he had never given anyone a reason to fear him, there were a few in town who did. Since Don and Ruth had no children of their own, they loved Jimmy as if he were theirs. Don called him Jim Bo and loved to tell everyone how Jim Bo had adopted him and Ruth.

Amanda went to the cupboard and got two more glasses. As she started to pour more milk, she said, "We brought enough cookies for everyone, Jimmy. You want a glass of milk too, don't you?"

Jimmy nodded. "Those cookies sure look good."

There wasn't much conversation in the room while everyone enjoyed the spicy cookies and the cold, sweet milk. As soon as Jenny had finished her cookie and glass of milk, her mother wiped her face and hands and put her on the floor.

Jenny immediately started pointing to the top of the refrigerator, saying "HoHo." She was pointing to her special toy at Aunt Ruth's house—a small wooden rocking horse. She loved to push on the backside of the horse and watch it rock back and forth.

"How 'bout we take that in on the wooden floor in the other room? It'll rock better in there," said Uncle Don.

"Me too?" asked Jimmy. Jimmy was fond of Jenny and loved to just watch her as she played.

"Sure," said Uncle Don. He reached on top of the refrigerator, retrieved HoHo, and gave it to Jenny. As the three headed off to the other room to play with the rocking horse, Amanda gathered the empty glasses and started to wash them.

* * *

The man in the car, who had been following Amanda and Jenny, had not been able to take his eyes off the little girl. When she and her mother disappeared inside, he sat and watched the house for some time. It didn't take long for him to pop the last pill he had with him. He washed it down with a beer from the six-pack in the backseat. Draining the remainder of the beer, he stumbled out of his car. He was soaked to the bone by the time he reached the back door. He stood to the side and watched everyone eating cookies and having a good time. He especially watched the little girl. When she left the room, he was desperate to see more of her. He opened the back door and walked in on the two women in the kitchen.

Amanda jumped when she heard the door open. At first she was merely startled, but she became alarmed when she realized the unwelcome guest was high. She looked into glassy eyes as he staggered toward her.

"Oh my God! What are you doing here?" Amanda looked first at the man and then at her aunt.

"I came to see the kid."

"Leave," she commanded. "Leave right now or I'll call Will."

Mocking her in a high-pitched voice he moved closer, "I'll call Will." Then he demanded, "I want to see the kid now!"

"Just get out!"

"Don't tell me what to do, you bitch!" He raised his hand to hit Amanda as Ruth let out a cry of alarm. The threat of not getting to meet the little girl frustrated him. Grabbing the first thing he saw lying on the counter—a knife—he waved it at the woman in the wheelchair. "Shut up and stay out of this!"

Amanda stepped between Ruth and the man. He swung the knife recklessly and nicked Amanda's cheek. Ruth screamed. Infuriated at the noise, he turned toward her. She screamed again. He had to make her stop screaming. Before even he realized what he was doing, he had plunged the knife into the woman's heart. As he pulled the knife back, Ruth gasped. Her body fell from the wheelchair to the floor. She was dead instantly.

Amanda was stunned. She instinctively started to kneel beside her aunt when the man came after her.

Everything had happened so quickly that by the time Don came rushing into the room, both women were lying together on the floor in a pool of blood. Shock hit Don when he saw the scene before him. He hesitated for just a second too long before he saw the knife coming toward him. Feeling as though he was moving in slow motion, Don turned and put his arm up to shield himself. He heard Jimmy call to him and managed to yell, "Jimmy run! Take Jenny and run!"

Jimmy became confused. Don's voice sounded odd. Instead of running away, Jimmy went into the kitchen. He saw a strange man attacking someone he loved. Jimmy started screaming, "Don! Don! I'll help you!" Jimmy didn't think of his own safety. He had to help Don. He ran at the man who was hurting his friend. He was so fast and came with such a force that the man dropped the knife when Jimmy's head rammed into his stomach. The man flew backward and slid across the floor. Jimmy stopped, picked up the knife, and began swinging at the air. He ran back to where Don was lying very still on the floor and stood straddled over his body. A sorrowful plea escaped his lips. He begged for Don to get up. He swayed back and forth in emotional pain, still holding onto the knife. The murderer was the one who was afraid now. All thoughts of the little girl were gone for the moment. He picked himself up off the floor and fled.

When the stranger ran out the back door, Jimmy would not abandon his protective watch over Don. He saw Jenny come into the room carrying her little rocking horse. She went to her mother's side. Jimmy wouldn't let anything else happen to Don, and he would take care of Jenny. He worried when Ruthie and Don would not answer him. He stopped yelling, but still stood over Don, protecting him and waving the knife.

~ 2 ~

By the time Will Barclay pulled his patrol car into the Shepman driveway, the rain had settled into a gentle shower. But earlier it had caused enough havoc to contribute to an accident that had kept Will tied up for a while. Will Barclay, Jimmy's brother, had been Shady Creek's county sheriff for over twenty years. He loved his job and was highly respected in the community. He was seventeen years older than his younger brother and had always helped his parents with Jimmy. He and his wife, Helen, were also rearing their own grandchild, four-year-old Daniel. Daniel's parents had been killed in a tragic automobile accident two years earlier. It had been raining that night too. Will hated rainstorms.

He waited a few minutes and decided against honking — he was going to have to go inside to get Jimmy. He got out of the patrol car and ran to the back door. He knocked, stepped inside, and saw his brother wielding a large kitchen knife and straddling Don Shepman's lifeless body. There was blood everywhere. He heard Amanda Preston's little girl crying softly. As he looked at the child, he couldn't believe what he was seeing. She was on the floor beside her mother's body, patting her on the back, attempting to comfort her. But Will could see that Amanda was also dead.

"My God," he murmured. He was in a state of disbelief as he looked around the room. Jimmy still swayed back and forth. "Jimmy, its okay. Jimmy. You're okay now, Jimmy," Will repeated, trying to keep his voice calm.

Jimmy's pathetic reply was, "Ruthie...Don." Tears slid down his cheeks.

Will started talking to his brother in a soothing voice. He approached Jimmy very slowly, took the knife away from him, and laid it on the counter. Next he reached down to check Don's pulse, but he knew before he did that Don was dead. He quickly checked the two women for any signs of life. Not finding any, he gently led his brother away from Don. Jenny turned her head toward her mother, making air-sucking sounds that told him she had been crying for some time. He couldn't believe the little girl wasn't hurt. He moved toward her, and when he picked her up in his arms she began to wiggle and squirm. She wanted to get back to her mother's side.

"It's okay, little one. Mommy's sleeping," he managed to lie. He knew this child. What was her name? Jimmy was standing beside Don again. Will knew he had to get the little girl and Jimmy out of this mess before he did anything else. He held the wriggling child in one arm, putting his other around Jimmy as he pulled him out the back door into the rain. Because of the rainstorm, the day had already gotten dark. Will looked at the neighbor's houses, but there were no lights on inside. The child in his arms was trying to tell him something.

"Bo," she whispered with chattering breath. Her skin was so cold. She turned her head into Will's shoulder and started crying again.

Will shuddered. He suddenly remembered her name. It was Jenny. She couldn't say Jimmy yet, so she called his brother Bo, for Jim Bo. What on earth had happened here tonight? What had this child seen? What had Jimmy done? Jimmy would never hurt Don and Ruth—would he? Will needed to take care of Jimmy and Jenny. He put Jimmy in the car and sat the child on Jimmy's lap. Jimmy hugged the struggling little girl and immediately started rocking back and forth, whimpering, "Don, I'm sorry Don."

Will had to get these two out of here. His mind was racing. He would take Jimmy home first, and then he would take the child to her grandparents. When he was sure Jimmy and the little girl were safe, he would come back and start acting like the sheriff again. Oh God, how would he be able to tell Richard and Barbara Preston what had just happened to their daughter?

* * *

When Will walked into his parent's house, Clara and Harold Barclay knew that something horrific had happened. Will, Jimmy, and Jenny were all soaked to the bone from the rain. Jimmy's clothes were spattered with blood, and he was so agitated that it took all three adults in the room to calm him down. Thankfully Jenny had been quiet when they came into the house. She was still clutching the toy rocking horse she had been playing with earlier in the evening. Will had put her on the couch where she had curled up into a sofa pillow and cried herself to sleep.

Jimmy finally calmed down enough that his father took him upstairs to his room. Will and Clara stepped into the kitchen so they would not wake the sleeping little girl. Clara finally said, "Okay, Will, tell me what happened."

"I can't tell you everything, Mom. I have to get back to the Shepman house. Someone killed Amanda Preston and Ruth and Don tonight." Clara gasped and sat down firmly in a chair, afraid of what else Will would say. He continued slowly, choosing carefully what to tell his mother. "I found Jimmy and Jenny there. I have to sort this out. Just take care of Jimmy, and I'll let you know what I can, when I can. Just don't say anything to anyone for now."

Looking as though the weight of the world were on top of him, he hugged his mother and held her for a moment. Then he went into the other room to get Jenny. But when he entered the front room, the first thing he saw were muddy, bloody footprints. What he didn't see sent a cold fear up his back—he didn't see Jenny. "Oh my God, what now?" Will ran to the door and saw two taillights disappearing down the street.

He stood for a long time just staring at the black hole where the taillights had gone. Everything in his body was screaming at him to go after that car, but he couldn't think. He felt relief. Now he was certain that Jimmy had done nothing wrong. But he had lived with small town prejudices against his brother all his life. This was getting much too complicated. Jenny's voice from the scene at the Shepman's backdoor was still echoing in his head. The fact that she kept pointing at Jimmy and saying "Bo, Bo" also haunted him. God he hated himself at this moment, but he had to protect Jimmy. He had seen no one else around the house. Jimmy's prints were all over that knife—the knife that he had to get rid of before anyone else saw that horrible scene. Will knew in his heart that Jimmy could never hurt Don or Ruth. But Will loved Jimmy and couldn't think about anything except protecting his brother right now. The others were dead. Chances were good that he would never find the car anyway. Since Jenny was now missing, her abduction could explain a motive for the horrendous murders. Maybe it was Jenny's father. After all, Amanda had told no one, including her parents, who Jenny's father was.

Will thought his head was going to explode. He needed time to think. He needed to get rid of that knife. Then he would call in the state police, and they could deal with looking for Jenny. No one needed to know that his brother was ever in that house tonight. His parents would go along with anything he asked them to if they thought it would protect Jimmy. He headed back into the house to talk to his mom again. Then he could do what he had to do at the Shepman house before he let anyone else know what had happened.

~ 3 ~

By the time the state authorities arrived in Shady Creek, the crime scene had been so compromised that they knew their hands were tied.

"Half the people in this damned town have trampled through the house looking for the missing kid. The other half are hysterical with fear!"

"That stupid sheriff needs to have his freaking head examined!"

Ray, Shady Creek's one and only deputy, had overheard the exchange between the two state officials on the scene. If he had not felt so loyal to his boss, he would have agreed. But he had been the one who had to stay with the bodies while Will told his best friends what had happened. He had seen the look on Will's face when he'd come back to the house and announced that Jenny was missing. Until then everyone thought Jenny was at her grandparent's house. So when she was not found in the house with the victims, pandemonium broke loose.

The story of what had happened in Shady Creek spread like a prairie fire on a windy day. People showed up and turned over every rock and leaf in the town looking for the missing child. The rain had stopped, but it was dark and the going was slow. The state police set up roadblocks in and out of town, and the news was broadcast on bulletins.

There just were no leads. The father of the child would have been notified and probably would've been a suspect, but no one except the mother had known who he was. Will tried to fend off some of the questions that were thrown at Richard and Barbara Preston—questions about Ruth and Don—questions about Amanda. Who was the father of the missing child? Did they have any enemies at all?

Barbara shut down completely, not unwilling to answer, but unable. Richard was so concerned for his wife and his missing grandchild that he thought he might lose his mind. He tried to stay strong, but the horrors of the day overwhelmed him.

Richard knew he couldn't leave Barbara alone. However he had to do something or he thought he might blow up. He called Barbara's closest friend, Rita McGee. When he told Rita what had happened and asked her to come over, she rushed to Barbara's side. As soon as she arrived, Richard knew that Rita could give Barbara more comfort than he could. He took off to find his granddaughter, only to be told he needed to stay put in case someone else found her. But Richard was not one to be told what to do.

"You can lock me in jail, but that's the only way you're going to keep me from looking for Jenny." He turned and walked out into the night.

Flashlights were everywhere, and people were talking in hushed voices. Even though the state authorities needed people to help look for the missing child, they didn't want any more people out milling around without direction. But this was one of their own—the people of Shady Creek would look for Jenny no matter what a few state authorities said. The town desperately needed to find the little girl. However all the praying and all the searching came up empty. They did not find the missing child or any trace of her. Richard came home shortly after daybreak, exhausted and defeated.

* * *

Randy Kingman awoke with a penetrating scream assaulting his fuzzy brain. He always hated coming off a high anyway, but what was that screeching noise? Looking in the direction of the offense, his brain cleared quickly. Stabbing pains were shooting through his skull and he started gagging with the smell that was emitting from the backseat—the same backseat where all the noise was coming from. "What the hell is going on? What have I done? What the Sam hell have I done?" He turned and bellowed into the backseat. "Shut up!" Jenny stopped screaming only long enough to look into Randy's eyes, draw another healthy amount of air into her lungs, and start screaming again. Randy started pounding the seat beside him bellowing even louder, "Shut up!" Jenny's eyes widened, but her scream turned into a soft whimper.

Randy opened bloodshot eyes and looked around. He was parked in a cornfield, the car hidden from the road. He looked down to see he was wearing blood-soaked clothes. He got out of the stinking car, walked around it, then climbed onto the hood, making a huge dent. Immediately to his left was a dirt road. About fifty yards to his right was an irrigation ditch. He climbed off the hood and opened the trunk, where most of his belongings were jammed helter-skelter. He dug around for a suitcase. Pulling one out of the car, he found a pair of jeans and two T-shirts.

First he stripped off his own clothes. Then he pulled Jenny from the backseat, stripping her stinking clothes off too. He was going to just throw the clothes into the field, then thought about it and bundled the dirty, shitty, bloody clothes together and stuffed them into the trunk. Jenny had turned up the volume again. "Shut up kid, or I'll give you something to scream about," he threatened, while twisting her arm. Jenny let out a little shriek. "Jenny and Daddy are going for a swim, little girl." Jenny stopped screaming but started struggling in Randy's arms.

Holding the squirming child tightly, he slid himself and Jenny into the irrigation ditch. He caught his breath as they hit the water. Randy had no idea that water could be so cold and still be in a liquid state. Jenny stopped struggling. Now she was clinging. Her teeth started chattering, yet she was trying to lick the water off her hands and arms. Randy reasoned she must be thirsty. He cupped his right hand in the icy bath and took a drink. Then he cupped up some for Jenny. She sucked up some of the water and immediately started shaking violently.

"Okay, baby doll, we'll get out of here before we freeze our asses off. At least you smell a little better now."

There had not been much rain here—wherever here was—and the temperature was rising quickly as the summer sun beat down. Both Jenny and Randy were dry by the time they got back to the car. He put a T-shirt over Jenny and put her in the front seat. Then he quickly dressed himself and got in behind the wheel.

A motor starting in the distance broke the quiet of the day. Randy thought he'd better get out of this field before some hick farmer spotted him and called the cops. That was the last thing he wanted. Flattening more cornstalks than he had when he had driven into the field, he retraced the path and found his way back to the road. Finally on the road again, he headed in the direction he thought was east. "Jenny, how do you think you'd like to live in Chicago for just a little while?" No answer—just big wide deep green eyes staring at him. "You're going to live with your daddy now."

Jenny kept looking toward the back of the car. She wanted something. Randy looked around and saw the dumb rocking horse that she'd had in her arms the night before at the sheriff's house. She had held it close while she slept on the couch. My God! He suddenly remembered what he had done. Why had he been so stupid to walk in and take the girl? "Why couldn't I just have left without you kid? Why the hell did I think I had to see you anyway?"

Jenny slowly screwed up her face and whimpered, "Mommy." Tears were forming again. Randy had no idea how such a little kid could have so many tears. He was trying to think of what to do next. He couldn't remember everything that had happened the night before. He remembered arguing with Amanda Preston about seeing his kid. He remembered snatching the kid. He had heard about her when she was born. Amanda had written to tell him he had a little girl named Jenny. He had not wanted anything to do with either one of them at the time, but then something happened. He just wanted to see what his kid looked like. Yesterday, before he went on with his new life, he decided he was going to see her. When he watched her walking down the street, he felt strongly that he needed to meet her. What if he never got another chance? But all he remembered was grabbing her at the sheriff's house. God, where did all that blood come from? And how in the hell did he end up in the middle of a cornfield?

Randy reached over and flicked on the radio. He fiddled with the dial until he heard a popular song. Just as he was about to find another station, the announcement came over the airwaves,

"We interrupt this program to bring you the latest bulletin on the murders last night in the small town of Shady Creek, Kansas. The police still have no clues as to motive for the murders and have no knowledge of the whereabouts of a two-year-old girl, Jenny Preston. Her mother, Amanda Preston, and an aunt and an uncle, Ruth and Don Shepman, were all murdered last night in the Shepman home. The police are searching the area for the little girl, who may have wandered off. However they are not ruling out the possibility of a kidnapping. They are asking anyone with any information about the murders or the disappearance of the little girl to call the Kansas State Police. Now back to our regular programming."

When Randy slammed on the brakes, Jenny flew to the floorboards. She started wailing again. It took Randy a full minute to pick her up to see if she was okay. What the hell was he doing? All that blood all over his clothes! He didn't remember anything except arguing with Amanda to see his kid. He stared at Jenny who already was forming a huge, red goose egg on her forehead. He looked around, hoping he was in a bad dream.

A trail of dust was kicking up on the other end of the road, so he quickly put Jenny back into the seat beside him, buckling her in this time. He drove down the lonely road toward the rusty pickup truck headed in their direction. The driver waved the standard country acknowledgment of one raised finger with his hand on the wheel. Randy waved back. But as soon as the pickup went past and the dust had cleared, he stopped the car. The full impact of what he, Randolph Kingman, might have done hit him. He opened the door and hardly had made it out of the car before he started puking his guts out. His clothes had been covered in blood, and he couldn't even remember what the hell had happened. At that moment he couldn't figure out why he had decided to go back to Shady Creek in the first place.

Randy Kingman had grown up in Shady Creek, where he thought his life was about as boring and mundane as it could get. When he finally went away to Kansas State University in Manhattan, he felt good about himself for the first time. Then he came home his freshman year at Christmas, excited to see his parents. They gave him the news that they were splitting up. His world fell apart. He had no idea his parents were having trouble with their marriage. Shortly after his

Christmas break ended, his dad left for the West Coast and his mom headed back to her hometown in Idaho. Randy didn't feel like he had a home at all anymore.

He started experimenting with drugs and occasionally came back to Shady Creek to see Amanda. The Prestons wouldn't let Amanda date a college boy. She was seventeen at the time. But Amanda found ways to sneak away to meet him. Then she got pregnant. When she asked Randy what they should do, he said he could get the money together for an abortion. Amanda told Randy he could go screw himself.

Randy didn't care about anyone else right then. He managed to stay in school, even though he began doing some hard partying. But the drugs and booze only seemed to make Randy lonelier. Out of the blue he called Amanda when Jenny was almost a year old. He begged her to see the baby. She refused. She told him that no one, including her parents, even knew who the father was. It was better if they never saw each other again. After all he had wanted her to get rid of "it."

Randy felt so alone and unconnected to anyone. Then he met Katherine Marshall. She saw something in Randy that no one else seemed to. With Katherine, Randy felt as if he could once again have a relationship with someone. So after he graduated he'd headed to where Katherine was, Chicago. He interviewed with several companies and landed a promising job that was to start at the beginning of the month. He went back to Kansas to pick up some of his things and decided to celebrate with just a couple of pills—for old time's sake. With his brain fuzzed up, he'd gotten a whacked out idea to swing by Shady Creek one last time before heading east again. Then he'd popped a couple more pills before he got to the quiet little town. He hadn't thought he was high—just buzzed. He must have gotten some bad stuff. What the hell had he done?

Randy didn't know how long he had been standing in the middle of the road puking and wondering what kind of shit he had become. He pulled himself back into the real world and vowed that he would never pop another pill no matter how lonely and pathetic his life became. He looked at his daughter in the car. She was buckled into the front seat, sitting in his dirty T-shirt. Her arm was still red where he had twisted it earlier, and she had a good-sized knot on her forehead. She turned and once again tried to reach between the seats into the back of the car. He looked down and saw the pathetic little rocking horse lying on the floor. It had a nasty reddish brown stain on it. Good God, what had his daughter seen? He handed the horse to Jenny. He was rewarded with a weak smile, a smile that changed the direction of his life forever.

~ 4 ~

Amanda Preston's remains were the last of the three bodies to be buried. The funeral for three people had truly been the most unusual this town had ever witnessed. Barbara had insisted that Ruth's, Don's, and Amanda's services be combined. "They all died together," she pleaded. "Please let us mourn them together."

It posed a problem because none of the churches in Shady Creek were large enough to handle all the mourners, so the service was held in the high school gymnasium. Ruth and Don belonged to the Presbyterian Church, while Amanda was a Methodist, so ministers of both churches spoke at the service. The funeral home only had one hearse, so they borrowed two others. When the three hearses pulled out of the school parking lot to head for the cemetery, the streets were lined with mourners. Most of the businesses in the town were closed for the day. Almost everyone in Shady Creek knew at least one of the deceased.

Richard and Barbara Preston held each other's hands as they sat under the tent beside their daughter's coffin.

After the three interments, the minister announced the customary lunch that would be served for family and friends in the school gymnasium. Many of the women from the churches had already left to help serve the mounds of food that people had brought. The handful of those who could not go to the lunch had already offered their heartfelt condolences. Richard heaved a huge sigh and told Barbara it was time to go.

Barbara didn't know how she had managed to make it to this day. When Will had come to their home to tell them of the tragedy, she had thought she was in some kind of horrible nightmare. She couldn't seem to wake up. Everything moved in slow motion for the next three days. Rita had helped her pick out the clothes for Amanda, Ruth, and Don. It was also Rita who had stayed with her when Richard saw to other arrangements. Not until this moment did she realize what a good job he had done. As they rode in the limousine to the gym now, she finally looked into the eyes of the man who had been a rock for her. "Thanks, Richard," was all she could say.

"It's okay, we'll make it, hon," he answered and then added with determination, "and we'll find Jenny soon."

Barbara had such a hole in her heart at the moment that she couldn't deal with the thought that the killer might have taken their little grandchild. The uncertainty of not knowing what had happened to Jenny was almost unbearable. She looked out the window so that she wouldn't see any more of the pain on Richard's face. Then she realized that they were back at the gym already. Their friends and neighbors would give them as much comfort as was possible, and then they would go home to their own families. As much as they had helped her, they could not possibly understand what she was feeling right now.

She had never known hate before, but she knew it now. It was directed toward an unknown evil. It produced a rage that she never thought possible for herself. One minute she felt the rage and the next she felt fear. But the pain was always there. She didn't know which emotion would come out next. But she did know that it was time for her to start helping Richard deal with his grief too. They walked together into the gym, into all the hugs and tears that helped them get through this day.

As Sheriff Barclay finished directing the funeral procession, he was having a lot of his own mixed emotions. He gave the appearance of being cold sometimes so that others couldn't see his fear. He put on his sheriff's face now so that no one could read what he might be feeling. His wife, Helen, and his four-year-old grandson, Daniel, were with the mourners. When he had lost his son and daughter-in-law, he had almost fallen apart. Richard and Barbara Preston had helped him and Helen with their grief and anger and shown them what a blessing they had in Danny.

Now Richard and Barbara's daughter had been murdered, and they didn't even have their grandchild left to give them comfort. Will knew he was responsible for that. He had let whoever killed Amanda walk into his own parents' house and take that little girl away. And he had failed to follow those taillights. He felt guilty for everything that had happened that night. If only he hadn't been late. If only he had called Ray, his deputy, from the Shepman house. But that would have involved Jimmy, and Will knew he would never have been able to live with the consequences of that.

When Will walked into the crowded gymnasium, his grandson spotted him immediately and came running up to him.

"Granddad Will, I can't find Jenny," Danny said as Will squatted on his haunches to talk to the child. "Why are Barbara and Richard crying all the time?" he asked.

Will started to answer Danny, but something got caught in his throat instead. My God, he blamed himself for this mess. It was his job to protect the people of this town, and he had thoroughly screwed up. Could he live with himself if Jenny was never found?

~ 5 ~

Randy was sitting on the edge of a shabby bed in a seedy motel watching his daughter sleep. He had been driving on back highways, hitting every small town between Shady Creek, Kansas, and Chicago. It was taking him longer than he wanted, but it gave him time to think and allowed the drugs a little more time to get out of his system. As far as he knew, Amanda had never told anyone that he was Jenny's father, so he reasoned that he would not be under suspicion for taking her. He remembered following Amanda and Jenny to her aunt's house. He remembered confronting Amanda, and he remembered taking Jenny out of that idiot sheriff's house. But he couldn't remember anything else about that night. He was sure he hadn't killed anyone, but there had been blood all over his clothes. Where had that come from? And the radio had said there were three people killed.

Randy started shaking again. He had holed up in this crappy motel for a couple of days to flush all the drugs out of his system. While Jenny slept he had gone out for food and diapers. He had even gotten lucky and driven by a garage sale that had kids' clothes. They were boys' things, but they fit Jenny perfectly. The damned shakes were getting bad this time and tears came with them. He cried like a baby while the real baby in the room slept peacefully. He took a pillow and muffled his sobs so that he would not wake her. He felt like he was possessed, but he knew he could beat the demons inside him. He would change his life around, and he would finally grow up. But for right now, he sobbed into a grimy pillow and willed his brain to stop exploding. Finally, exhausted, he fell asleep.

Randy awoke the next morning with a small finger poking up one of his nostrils. Jenny actually giggled when he jumped. It was the first time he had heard her make a pleasant sound. He smiled at her and she smiled back. He took it as a good omen. It was time to venture out on the road again.

* * *

"You want another glass of milk, honey?" asked the waitress at the Pancake Kitchen. "You sure got one good-looking young man there, mister. I love those locks of curly hair."

Randy wasn't about to correct anyone if they thought Jenny was a boy. He had cut off some of the length of Jenny's hair and dressed her in the garage-sale clothes. No one had to know just yet that she was a girl.

"What's your name, honey?"

Jenny looked up and said nothing. The waitress was looking at Randy for an answer.

Randy quickly added, "Uh, this is Jay."

"Well, Jay, I'll get you another glass of milk, okay?"

Jenny looked up and rewarded the waitress with a smile. Randy realized he had been holding his breath for some time, not knowing just how much Jenny could say. Thank goodness she couldn't say her name yet. For now she was going to be known as Jay.

* * *

Now that the drugs were clearing from his system, the long drive was giving Randy time to think. He was supposed to start his new position in exactly one week. That gave him a week to sweet-talk Katherine Marshall. Randy had never told Katherine where he had grown up. He lied and told her that his family moved a lot when he was young. At least he had told her the truth when he said that his parents were divorced. He doubted that she cared a whit about his parents anyway, since they were not exactly in the same class that she grew up in.

The news he had heard on the radio gave him hope that he would never be found out. Randy formed his plan as he traveled the road with his daughter. He knew that Katherine had a weak spot in her heart for kids. He also knew that she would never be physically able to bear her own. Maybe he could convince Katherine that Jenny's mother had abandoned her. He thought that might endear him to Katherine even more. Randy looked over at Jenny. She was singing some gibberish and playing with that ugly, stupid rocking horse. He had picked up a cheap little doll for her at one of their stops, but she hung on to that damned rocking horse instead. At least it kept her quiet.

"Hey, kiddo, you and me are going to go meet your new mommy." He figured he had better get her used to the idea.

The lips curved upside down and the tears started to come. "Mommy" was all she said. She started crying softly.

"It's okay, kiddo," he tried to soothe her. "You'll like Katherine. You have a new name now too. Your name is Jay. No, that doesn't sound right. How about Jennifer? Yeah, that's right; Katherine will like Jennifer better than Jay. Hey Jennifer, you like your little horsey?"

"Ho," she said. "Ho," she repeated with a smile, looking at the stupid little horse. Oh well, it stopped the tears for a while anyway.

Randy smiled to himself, pleased with the fact that he could charm women, even little bitty women. He had no doubt that he could convince Katherine to accept Jennifer if it meant that she got him with the bargain. He came to an interstate and felt downright cocky enough to take it. Katherine might even like him better if she thought he was a loving father. The future looked bright. He started to whistle a tune. The child, now called Jennifer Kingman, smiled and started singing softly again.

* * *

As Randy Kingman was starting a new life with their granddaughter in Chicago, the Prestons were trying to cope with a life that now seemed empty. The first several years for both Richard and Barbara were filled with a deep grief mixed with the rage and fear they had felt right after the murders. They stopped talking things over with each other and withdrew into themselves. Then they started arguing frequently. On the fourth anniversary of the murder, Barbara and Richard fought bitterly over yet another trivial matter. Richard took a long walk to the graveyard. He talked to God in the place where he had buried his daughter. He ranted at God. How could He let such an injustice happen? He held none of his anger back. He didn't hear Barbara as she walked quietly up behind him. When she spoke to him he nearly jumped out of his skin.

"Richard, I love you," she said to his back. "But if we don't get a handle on this, it's going to destroy both of us. I can't live like this anymore, and I don't think you can either. How do we expect God to ever let us see Jenny again if we don't stop our hate long enough to even be kind to one another? I can't do this anymore. I have to let go." Barbara stopped long enough to catch her breath before she continued. "We fight—we argue—I don't even remember what our argument was about. We're fighting with one another because we can't fight with whoever killed our daughter. I am not going to let him destroy me too. It's been four long years, Richard. I will never quit hating what that maniac did to us and to our family. But I have to try to quit hating him so that I can start living again."

They both stood there in the silence of the graveyard for a long time. Finally Richard turned around slowly and looked at the woman he loved so dearly. He knew she was right, but he knew a higher power would have to intervene. Prayer had never come easily for Richard, and when it did, it was always a private matter. But this day he and Barbara prayed together for the hate to be lifted from their hearts. A new scab began to form. Another beginning was taking place. The rage did not go away, but it lessened. A heavy cloak of sorrow was made lighter as they walked back home together. They didn't even notice Will Barclay's car sitting on the other side of the roadway.

Will watched his friends. On every anniversary date of the murders, he saw them come here. He worried about them both. He had watched the most loving couple he knew be torn apart the last four years. He wanted to help them find their granddaughter in the worst way, but he had no leads. He was the only law enforcement that was still looking for the little girl. If only Amanda Preston had told someone who Jenny's father was, he might have had something to go on. He had always suspected the murderer might have been her father. If only Jimmy hadn't been there that night. If only Will hadn't been so stupid and incompetent to have let the murderer come back and get that little girl when he had her in his own parents' living room. God, he thought he was going to go crazy with that thought.

He had let Barbara and Richard down. He had let his town down. People were still afraid to be alone at night in Shady Creek. His guilt was overwhelming. He could hardly wait until he could go home and find some relief for a time in his favorite bottle of scotch.

SHADY CREEK, KANSAS
Present Time

~ 6 ~

A heavenly aroma greeted Julie when she crossed the threshold of the old house. It smelled like what? Ginger snap cookies! A bittersweet memory came with the smell, and then as quickly as the scent had reached her it was gone. She set her bags down, continuing into the parlor where a puff of cool air kissed her cheek. What strange, yet pleasant sensations, she thought.

"Let me take those bags upstairs for you," a masculine voice echoed off the walls. Julie had been so intrigued with the atmosphere of the house that she had almost forgotten Richard Preston, her new landlord, was standing behind her. He reached for the bags that she had dropped in the foyer as he continued, "We would have freshened the place up if we'd known you were coming today."

"My plans changed rather suddenly. I didn't realize myself that I would arrive this soon," Julie said with her back to the man.

"Barbara would've had fresh flowers and the works waiting for you by tomorrow afternoon. She always likes to have fresh flowers put in the house when someone new rents the place." Richard Preston was standing in the foyer with one of Julie's bags in each hand. When Julie turned around and he got a full look at her face, he quit talking and just stared. Julie was about to ask him if he was okay when he started talking again. But he seemed nervous all of a sudden and started talking faster. "This house belonged to her relations. They're all gone now, so we rent it. If we could find the right buyer, we'd sell it. But it's old and needs some updates. It's a good house though, kinda old fashioned. Shady Creek used to be a good-sized town in its day, but most of the younger generation moved on to the cities where the jobs are. You surprised me. What's a nice young thing like you doing in Shady Creek, if you don't mind my asking?"

Julie smiled and ignored the question as she turned and headed back out to the car. Not only could she not answer the question for her own safety, she wasn't sure herself just why she had chosen a little town in the middle of Kansas. But Shady Creek seemed like a good place to hide out until she could sort out her thoughts and feelings. It would be the last place on earth that Stan would look for her. She hadn't been able to think clearly for some time—she had been too afraid. She was looking forward to getting a good night's sleep without her husband by her side.

Julie was bent over the trunk of her car, trying to figure out what could stay in the car until the morning and what she needed now. She jumped as Mr. Preston broke the silence. "You need more help, Miss Hendricks?"

"Thank you, Mr. Preston. If you would be so kind as to take this box, I think I can manage the rest in the morning."

She handed over a box that contained towels, a blanket, and a set of sheets. She had stopped at a grocery store and picked up a few things before she had called Richard Preston to let her into the house.

Even though she had been planning an escape for a long time, Julie had left Chicago so quickly that she hadn't gotten everything she thought she might need. She had told no one that she was leaving. Her father had been out of the country on a business trip. When she went to her mother to complain about Stan, she received no support. She had felt her mother had betrayed her in this. She had told no friends about her plans. Ha! What friends? Stan had seen to it that she had no real friends of her own. When she could figure out what to do, she would think about calling her father.

Once she had made the decision to leave Stan, she had done some things that she had not thought herself capable of. She had met some characters she had never thought she would have to deal with. But those very characters had helped her find a new identity, for a very hefty price. She wasn't able to get her hands on as much cash as she would have liked, though. She knew that when Stan discovered that she had emptied her own small savings account, he would go ballistic. She started to tear up thinking of her messed up life. She questioned her own way of handling her problems, but she didn't know what else to do. Her thoughts were muddled. She needed time. She would deal with her problems tomorrow—problems like finding a job, returning the rental, combating her loneliness. She just needed a good night's sleep right now. Julie Hendricks, a.k.a. Jen Samuels did not trust anyone tonight except herself.

Julie jumped again as Richard Preston interrupted her thoughts. Had he said something else to her? Maybe he could tell she was some kind of fake? "Is there anything else I can help you with? Barbara will be sorry she missed you tonight, but she was at a meeting when you called. I think she's in charge of the program or something."

"Thank you, Mr. Preston. I'll be fine. If I need anything else, I'll call you tomorrow. I just want to take a hot shower and get some sleep."

"Well I got the hot-water heater hooked up yesterday, so you should be good to go then. I sure wish you would call me Richard, Miss Hendricks." Mr. Preston was looking at Julie as though he wanted to say more. Normally she would have been unsettled, but she didn't feel threatened by it, just strange—the same kind of strange she'd felt in the house a few minutes ago. Man, did she need sleep!

"I'll do that Richard, if you'll call me Julie."

"I sure can do that. Barbara will be so glad to have a young person in the house again. Now remember, we're the house on the corner. If you have any problems at all, just call or come on over."

Julie nodded and smiled as Richard Preston made his way down the front steps. As she locked the front door behind him, the enormity of everything she had done the past several days hit her. She went into the kitchen, put the milk she had purchased in the refrigerator, set the rest of the groceries on the counter, and turned out the light—everything else could wait for the morning. She turned off the downstairs lights and headed up the stairs toward the bedroom.

* * *

Yellow roses climbed the walls of the main bedroom. They were a little faded, yet charming. A bedside table with a lamp, a dresser with a mirror and small stool, and a white wrought iron double bed completed the furnishings. Julie got out the blanket and sheets. She soon had a comfy nest ready to crawl into. Darn! She had forgotten to get a pillow. But she was suddenly so tired, that it didn't matter. She kicked off her shoes, stripped down to her underwear, and was instantly reminded of why she was doing all of this when she looked at the bruises on her arms and legs. Turning off the lights, Julie lay down on the cool new sheets, grabbing the blanket to cocoon herself from her troubles. Her stomach growled, another reminder that she hadn't eaten since late morning. But she was too drained to care. Tears started flowing, and like a child she soon cried herself to sleep.

* * *

Richard Preston was shaken to his core when he left his new tenant. Normally quiet and reserved, he had babbled like a schoolboy around Julie Hendricks. He had to concentrate hard to try and act civil, and he knew he had gone overboard with talking. She probably thought him a doddering old fool, but his first look at her had brought back an intense pain that was as raw as the day his life had turned upside down twenty-two years ago. Amanda was all he could see when he looked at Miss Hendricks—the same high cheekbones, the chestnut hair, the way she walked, and those deep green eyes. When she spoke to him, memories blasted him like a furnace, memories of a day when he had lost part of his soul. Seeing Julie Hendricks made him remember how painful it had been.

As Richard approached his own house, he could see that Barbara was home. He stood on the porch for a long time, trying to calm himself before he went in. As he opened the door, he straightened his shoulders and put a smile on his face. "You beat me home," he announced when Barbara looked up from the book she was reading.

"And just where have you been?" she asked as she accepted the kiss he placed on her lips.

"Well," he hesitated, "that Hendricks woman—Julie—called. She got into town earlier than we expected, so I let her in the house."

"Oh shoot! I wanted to freshen it up and put some flowers in for a welcome, and…" Barbara slowed her words and asked, "Richard is something wrong?"

"What makes you think something's wrong?"

"Richard Arnold Preston, after all these years together I can read you like a book. What's wrong?"

Sighing heavily Richard knew he would have to talk to Barbara about Julie Hendricks. He wanted to give her a little warning before she met the girl. Richard went over to the family pictures above the buffet table. "Barbara, we need to talk about the new tenant."

Barbara couldn't read Richard's expression now, and she was alarmed when he reached for Amanda's picture. "Richard, please just tell me what's wrong."

With a heavy heart Richard started to tell Barbara everything that had happened. Then he added, "Barbara, I think the girl is running away from some kind of trouble. But, Barbara," Richard cleared his throat, "Barbara, she is the spitting image of our Amanda." Richard turned his face into Barbara's and she could feel the pain he was feeling. An all-too-familiar sadness enveloped them. They held each other for a while. Each gave the other a little more strength to deal with their memories.

* * *

Only the gentle rustle of the cottonwood could be heard from the open window in the Preston bedroom. A fresh wisp of air came through the window along with a soft glow from the moon. Both Barbara and Richard lay awake for a long time that night. Each had their own thoughts of Amanda and Jenny—the daughter and granddaughter they had loved and lost that tragic day so long ago. The memories were as vivid as if it had happened yesterday.

Richard slipped out of bed when Barbara's rhythmic breathing told him she was finally asleep. He went out to the back porch and sat in the moonlight for a long time, trying to reason that a lot of people looked like someone else. After Amanda had been murdered, he had often thought he saw her likeness in others. Tonight was different though. Tonight the similarity had not faded.

~ 7 ~

Julie awoke to a cacophony of extremely busy birds outside her bedroom window. Crawling from her own nest, she searched for her toothbrush to erase the dry hay bale she must have eaten last night. Oh yeah, she hadn't eaten any dinner. Her nose was stuffed up, and the crick in her neck would remind her all day of the importance of picking up a pillow. "That's what you get for allowing yourself those tears," she thought aloud. A quick peek in the mirror made her want to go back to bed. "Oh, no," came a low moan. Julie splashed cold water on her swollen eyes. "You're going to start your new life looking like you had a bad night at the bar!" she said to the reflection of the new Julie Hendricks. Forcing a generous smile for the mirror, she was determined to push back the fear that she saw just under the surface. She searched through the box Mr. Preston had carried up the stairs for her last night. She remembered packing towels and a bar of soap somewhere.

* * *

Julie was always amazed at how a shower could renew her courage to face a new day. Taking a clean pair of jeans from her suitcase, she found her little toy rocking horse, HoHo, tucked away in the corner. It was the only sentimental thing she'd allowed herself to pack. She had no idea why that rocking horse was so important to her, but she had had him since she was a child, and he made her feel better every time she held him. She walked over to the dresser and placed HoHo there. As she turned back to her suitcase for a clean white shirt, gooseflesh suddenly crawled up her arms. She swung back toward the dresser and stared at HoHo. He was rocking violently on the dresser. What on earth? As she timidly reached for the toy, it stopped rocking as abruptly as it had started. Her brow furrowed. She shook off the weird thoughts she was having. She must have bumped the little horse when she turned. "Get a grip!" she chastised herself. If she let her favorite childhood toy scare her, she would never have the courage to start anew. She glanced once more at HoHo as he sat quietly on the dresser, looking totally harmless. Walking out of the room she stopped in the hallway, turned, and peeked back in to look once more at the little horse sitting quietly on the dresser. "Okay, Julie Hendricks, everything is fine," she spoke in a determined but not so convincing voice. She straightened her shoulders to take on her new life.

Julie descended the stairs feeling comfortable in her jeans. She used to wear jeans all the time, but even designer jeans had never quite suited Stan. Stan liked dresses, and he insisted she wear them. Well Stan wasn't here now to tell her what to do, and she needed to concentrate on herself and not on Stan. She was in control of her life again. It actually felt strange. It had been a long time since she felt in control of anything. She hoped she wouldn't have to worry about Stan for now. She doubted that Mr. Stanley Samuels III would even blink at a town like Shady Creek.

At the bottom of the stairs, Julie was greeted with the same aroma of deliciousness that she had smelled the night before. And once again the odor was gone as suddenly as it had arrived. It gave her a sense of both anxiety and warmth. She was transported back to memories of her childhood. Maude, her mother's housekeeper, had always had cookies and milk waiting for her when she came home from school. It was Maude who had asked her about her day and fixed her hurts when she fell off her bike. When she was in third grade, Maude was the person she'd told about Mark Simpson trying to kiss her at recess. Maude's hugs had always been full of unconditional love. She had longed for that feeling from her mother, and though she never doubted that her mother loved her, she never felt warmth from her. Maude had been her true friend and mentor, and Julie had truly loved her. She shook her head. She hadn't thought about Maude in a long time, and she couldn't imagine why she was thinking of her now.

Walking from the hallway into the kitchen, Julie found everything exactly as she had left it the night before. She started searching in the cupboards. Barbara Preston had told her on the phone that the last renter had left a few dishes in the house, and she was welcome to use them. She found four dinner plates, three cereal bowls, two coffee mugs, and eight mismatched glasses. She reached for a glass. It had a thick rim with writing etched on its side. It looked as though it may have held jelly at one time. How quaint. "Guess I won't be drinking out of crystal stemware for a while," she chuckled.

She desperately needed a cup of coffee. Oops! She had bought coffee, but had no coffeemaker. Her stomach growled. She poured cereal in one of the bowls, and just as she was about to pour milk on it, she grasped the fact that she had no spoons. "So this is what independence feels like," she grumbled as she grabbed a handful of the dry cereal. She poured her milk into a glass that had etched grapes on the side of it. What a pitiful breakfast for a person who loved to cook. She sat down on a stool by the counter and assessed the room for a minute. She didn't even have a cup of coffee to get her day started, but she didn't have anyone yelling at her either. A smile and shaky satisfaction settled over her. She felt scared, lost, liberated, and in need of that coffee.

Julie went to her purse for a pen. Good grief, she didn't have any paper. She searched through a couple of drawers and found a small notepad with an ad for the local lumberyard on it. She wrote: coffeemaker—pillow—spoons—sugar. "You can do this," she said to herself. Now all she had to do was believe it.

Being Julie Hendricks might take some getting used to. All her life as Jennifer Kingman, she couldn't remember a time that she had ever had to be on her own before. She grabbed another handful of cereal and took a drink of milk. Even in college, all she'd had to do was call Maude whenever she needed anything. How she wished Maude were still alive. She would be the one person Julie could call for advice. Maude had always been there for her. If only she could relate so well with her mother. Tears threatened every time she thought about her last conversation with Katherine. She had tried to explain that she was becoming afraid of Stan. She'd tried to tell Katherine how worthless he made her feel and how his temper would flare at the slightest disagreement. Katherine had looked at her daughter with disbelief and told her that all marriages had rough spots.

"It's time you grew up a little, Jennifer," she had said.

"But, Mother, Stan just seems so angry. I can't seem to do anything that pleases him."

It hadn't started out that way. Stan had praised her in almost everything she had done the first year of their marriage. He had been the perfect husband. Stan was the only one who had ever called her Jen, and she had loved it. At first it irritated her mother, but Stan had convinced her that Jen was only a pet nickname reserved just for him.

"Mrs. Kingman, she will always be your Jennifer, but to me, she will always be my Jen," he had told her mother. And Stan was nothing if he wasn't charming.

Julie herself did not know when Stan had changed toward her. She just knew that instead of praising what she did, he complained. And then the complaints turned into insults. He demanded to know her whereabouts every minute of every day. He embarrassed her in front of her friends, to the point that she no longer had any close friends. The last several months he had even started going shopping with her. He picked out her clothes and insisted that she wear only what he chose. But when Jennifer tried to talk to her mother about Stan's behavior, Katherine stood up for Stan.

"When your father gets back from his Australian trip, you can talk with him."

Jennifer had left her mother's house doubting everything about herself. Maybe Katherine was right. She went home thinking she would just try harder. But Stan was already home. He met her at the door. It seems her mother had called him and expressed her concern that maybe Jennifer was going into a depression. Stan was furious.

For the next month, the only time Stan would talk to her was when they were around others. He complained about everything she did. If she tried to talk to him, she was met with cold stares. She finally worked up the courage to tell him she thought they needed to separate for a time. Stan made her pay for that suggestion.

"I will kill you before I ever let you leave me. Do you hear me Jen? I will kill you."

His eyes told her he was not making an idle threat. Jen knew that she needed to be very careful with what she said and did, and in whom she confided. She felt betrayed by her own mother. Her father had called her one day when Stan was home. She didn't dare say anything while Stan was with her. She had tried to call her father several times when Stan wasn't around and could never get through to him. He was usually gone on another of his many business trips.

With the constant belittling, she started doubting herself in everything she did. She knew she had to get away from Stan so that she could think clearly and without fear. That was when she started planning a way to escape until—

Julie's phone interrupted her thoughts. She stared at it as though it were a bomb about to explode. She had forgotten to turn it off. Even though it was one of those pay-by-the-minute phones and she had given the number to no one, she panicked. She had only used it to call the Prestons. She didn't know much about technology, but she thought she remembered news stories of people being found by leaving their cell phones on. She walked over and turned it off and threw the phone on the counter as though it had shocked her.

She really didn't think that Stan would go to the police to try to find her; but if he told her mother that she was missing, she knew Katherine would try to find her. "Okay, don't panic. Today you are going to get rid of the rental and look for a job." Julie grabbed the last handful of cereal, emptied the glass of milk and squared her shoulders. Richard Preston had told Julie that if she needed anything to come over. She grabbed her purse and headed out the door toward the Preston house. The first thing she needed was to find a cup of coffee.

~ 8 ~

Barbara awoke to the smell of fresh coffee. Normally an early riser, she quickly dressed and met Richard coming down the hallway carrying her favorite mug.

"I thought I'd bring you a cuppa joe while you dressed. Looks like I'm too late."

"Better watch out. I could get used to that kind of luxury," she quipped as she kissed him for the first time of the day. They walked into the kitchen together and, like a synchronized team, they silently prepared their breakfast. Richard went to the fridge and grabbed juice and milk, while Barbara set out the juice glasses and cereal bowls. As she poured cereal into both bowls she said, "I think I'll bake something to share with our new tenant today."

"Barbara, I think you should prepare yourself for the likeness of the girl."

Turning to face her husband she said gently, "I trust your judgment Richard, but I need to meet her myself. Neither one of us is getting any younger, and we can't afford to live our nightmare over again."

They finished their breakfast in silence. Barbara picked up her mug, walked over to the window, and looked out. Richard heard a gasp from her as she set the mug down hard on the corner of the counter. She was shaking her head as Richard rushed to her side. He glanced out the window and saw Julie Hendricks walking up the front walk.

"Barbara, are you okay?"

Nodding her head, she grabbed the back of a chair for support. "It's Miss Hendricks, isn't it?"

Richard's eyes confirmed her guess. Seconds later the doorbell rang. "I'll let her in. Are you sure you're okay?"

Barbara nodded once again.

Julie was standing at the door looking much better than she had the night before. Her eyes were a little puffy, but she didn't have the scared rabbit look anymore. Richard opened the door with as friendly a welcome as he could muster, "Good morning, Julie. How was your first night in Shady Creek?"

"It was a wonderful night, but I was wondering if you could tell me where I could get a quick cup of coffee in town. I didn't bring a coffeemaker with me."

Richard looked over his shoulder to make sure Barbara was okay. "That's an easy one. C'mon in. We've got the best cuppa joe in town. Barbara is anxious to meet you."

"Oh, wonderful," smiled Julie. "It will be so much easier to deal with my morning if I have my caffeine fix."

Julie stepped through the front door as Barbara came toward her with an outstretched hand. "Welcome to Shady Creek and our home. I hope you like it here." Barbara put her arm around Julie and led her in the direction of the kitchen.

Julie's immediate reaction was a feeling that she had met Maude's double in her new life. Barbara even looked a little like Maude, except for her hazel eyes that held both sadness and a sparkle. Her hair was seasoned with a sprinkling of salt and light brown pepper cut short and wispy. She walked with grace even though she carried a few extra pounds around her middle. It gave her an approachable quality somehow.

The Preston kitchen was as inviting as they come. Barbara reached for another mug and began pouring Julie a cup of coffee. "Did you have anything for breakfast?"

"Breakfast has been taken care of, but the coffee smells heavenly. You are a life saver Mrs. Preston."

"I don't do too well without my coffee in the morning either. How's the moving going? And please, call me Barbara."

"Okay, Barbara. And I'm Julie." Julie instinctively liked this woman. "I don't have much to unpack. Guess I need a little information though."

Richard came into the room, looked anxiously at Barbara, and visibly relaxed when he saw the look of ease on her face. He sensed that if it were possible at all for these two women to become friends, it would be good for Barbara. Julie's likeness to Amanda didn't seem to bother Barbara once she got over the initial shock of meeting her. Wanting to give the two more time to get acquainted, Richard decided to take a long walk. He bent over Barbara and gave her a peck on the cheek. "I'll be back at lunchtime and I have my cell with me if you need anything. Have a good chat, ladies."

Julie was truly enjoying the coffee and Barbara's conversation. She wanted a friend so badly. She was already feeling the need to confide in someone, but knew she would not be able to do that. After all, Stan had turned on her without warning, and her own mother had…she wasn't sure what her mother had done. Right now she had to depend on Julie Hendricks. Her money wouldn't last forever, and she was concerned that if she didn't get rid of the rental car, not only would it drain her budget fast, she was afraid it might help Stan find her.

"What kind of information can I help you with, dear?" asked Barbara as she sat down across from Julie at the kitchen table.

"I was so tired when I drove in last night that I didn't really pay much attention, but when I drove down First Street, I noticed a few shops."

Barbara chuckled softly. "That was downtown Shady Creek, my dear. We have two banks, a small grocery store, a pharmacy, a hardware store, an antiques store, a furniture store, and a café. Oh and then out on the outskirts of town we have a Pizza Hut and an old folks home and the Dairy Crème. On the other side, on the highway, we have an implement dealer and a nice lumberyard."

Barbara took a sip of coffee and continued on as Julie sat there, amazed. Barbara went on to describe Shady Creek down to the last detail, throwing both the good and the not-so-good together. It was apparent that she loved and accepted it all the same. She talked about the churches— three in all—and the school. She ended with, "I have lived in Shady Creek most of my life, except when I was young and went away to college. My, that was ages ago. But I haven't let you get a word in. Was there something specific you have questions about?"

"Is there a place to return a car rental?"

"Oh dear, I don't think so. But Salina surely has a place. If you want to drive over there, maybe I could go over too and pick you up. I always like to go shopping there."

"I wouldn't want to inconvenience you, but I really can't afford to keep it much longer. I'm also going to need to find a job as soon as possible."

Barbara detected a small frown crossing Julie's face. She wanted desperately to help this girl, and she thought Richard was right about her being in some kind of trouble. She knew she had to be careful with what she asked. "When I talked to you on the phone, I thought maybe you were a writer or painter or something like that. What kind of job are you looking for?"

Julie's brow furrowed a bit more. "I guess I have to confess that I haven't had much experience in the job market."

"Well there's not much of a job market in Shady Creek," Barbara said as a thought came to her. "Can you cook?"

"I love to cook. But I don't know if I could handle a restaurant or café or anything like that."

"Pour yourself another cup of coffee, and I'll be right back." Barbara grabbed the phone and went into another room where Julie could hear her speaking to someone. Julie was standing by the back window admiring a lovely flower garden when Barbara walked back into the kitchen with a smile on her face. There was that instant reminder of Maude again.

Barbara was now holding her hand over the end of the phone. "How about an interview this afternoon? I have a friend who has a daughter who just opened a B&B in Shady Creek. She needs a cook for breakfast meals and occasionally for evening social engagements, like wedding receptions."

Julie was bobbing a yes answer as soon as she heard the question. Barbara smiled and said into the phone, "Here, I'll let you talk to her." She handed Julie the phone, whispering, "Her name is Willow."

Barbara watched the girl as she talked to Willow. She thought maybe Richard was right about her running away. Richard always had good instincts when it came to others. He was also right that this girl reminded her so much of her Amanda. As Julie got off the phone she looked delighted and excited.

"I have an interview at one o'clock. Thank you so much, Barbara."

"Believe me, if this works out you will be doing us all a favor. Willow hasn't had her B&B very long. She's really proud of that place—as she should be. I know she wants to make the breakfast part of the inn something really special though, and she...well, I guess I'd better let her tell you about that. She thought her mother, my friend Rita, was going to be able to help her more. I've even pitched in occasionally. Rita and I would rather tend our gardens though."

"I'd better get going, Julie said. "I have a few things to do before my interview with Willow."

Barbara had already drawn a map of the streets over to the Shady Creek Inn. It was only a few blocks away. Julie took the slip of paper from Barbara. "I don't know what to wear for an interview like this. I haven't brought much of a wardrobe with me."

"Well if I know Willow, what you have on is just about right." Barbara said, "We're a small town, and we care more about how you work than what you wear. Since she needs a cook, she might test you on the spot. Good luck, dear. Why don't you stop by when you get done and let me know what you think of the inn?"

~ 9 ~

Julie found a coffeemaker in the hardware store, a pillow in the furniture store, and settled for plastic spoons that she found in the grocery store. She also picked up a few more groceries but decided to keep everything at a bare minimum. Everyone she met was friendly and wanted to talk to her. They mostly asked where she was from and were interested in how long she would be in town. She certainly didn't blend in here. But she had to keep telling herself that no one here was a threat—they were just friendly and curious. It did unnerve her that some of the older people she met seemed a bit too inquisitive. Some did a double take. Did she look like she was a fake? She hadn't yet had to use any of her false identification that had cost her so much back in Chicago, so why would anyone question who she was?

Driving back to the house, she decided to do just a bit of exploring. Barbara had done such a good job of explaining the town to her that it didn't take long to see almost everything they had talked about. She finally ended up at the crest of the hill that looked down on the town and found herself by the hospital. It was a small one-story building with two doctors' offices at the end. Looking down on the town from the top of the hill, she could also see two of the three church steeples peeking through the treetops. She felt herself relaxing like a sightseer until she looked at her watch. Time to get herself home and freshen up—she needed this job.

* * *

Willow Johnson took a deep breath of the delicious smells coming from the kitchen downstairs. She had just placed fresh flowers in the Garden Room on the second floor. During the spring and summer months, she hoped to always have fresh flowers in each room to greet her guests when they arrived. Willow's mother, Rita McGee, was an avid gardener. She was helping Willow at the inn by managing the beautiful gardens that came with the huge old house. The gardens were an added bonus that furnished an assortment of flowers, vegetables, and herbs during the summer months. Rita loved keeping them up. She had also talked Willow into adding the enchanting gazebo that sat in the corner of the backyard.

Willow had always dreamed of running a bed and breakfast. When the Shady Inn went up for sale, she had talked her mother into helping her buy the place. It had taken her eight long months to get the five rooms into the shape she wanted them. She had done a room at a time while renting out the others. Now that she had everything finished to her satisfaction, she had also opened up the inn for special events.

Rita and Barbara Preston had been helping her get started, but it was time to hire some help and quit relying on her mother and her mother's friend. Willow was thrilled when Barbara had called and suggested she give Julie Hendricks an interview. After talking to her for only five minutes, Willow had put her in the kitchen to test her skills. She was hoping that Julie would work out. Her only other prospect was Myrtle Crow, who was seventy years old and bored with her life. Myrtle was a capable cook, but she liked to gossip more than she liked to cook. Willow thought she would probably drive guests away if she ever stuck her head outside the kitchen, and knowing Myrtle she would probably do just that.

So when Julie Hendricks walked in the door, she appeared to be heaven sent. Willow instantly liked Julie. If she could put on a good breakfast with the supplies Willow had in her kitchen, then she would be happy. The aromas floating through the vents right now gave her hope.

* * *

Julie hadn't cooked for anyone who appreciated it for a long time. If Stan had liked anything she cooked, he never let her know. When she'd made her appointment with Willow, she had been excited and very anxious at the same time. The Shady Inn was both enchanting and welcoming. It would be a lovely place to get up early and walk to every morning, since it was only a few blocks from her house. When she entered the inn and introductions were made, she wanted the job more than ever. Willow said the only way she could interview her was to see what she could do in the kitchen.

"If you can whip up a breakfast that my guests will remember with delight, with what I have in the kitchen, you're in the running for the job," Willow smiled and tried to put Julie at ease. "Since you aren't familiar with the kitchen, take your time finding things and let me know when you're done. Check-in is at four o'clock, so you have plenty of time before any guests arrive today. I'll be on the second floor getting a couple of rooms ready."

After acclimating herself to the inn's kitchen, Julie worked for almost two hours. She was ready for the verdict. The kitchen was well stocked with breakfast supplies. She could only hope she'd done them justice. She had prepared a fresh pot of coffee, a fruit yogurt parfait, a quiche, and French toast covered with pecans to be served with warm maple syrup. Tasting the quiche, she decided it was one of the best she had ever made. Thanks to Maude's patience with an inquisitive child, she had learned to cook some foods without a recipe. Just as she was getting ready to go find the inn's owner, Willow popped her head into the kitchen.

"I hope that tastes half as good as it smells. Are you ready to dazzle me?"

"I can only hope," replied Julie.

Willow sat at the head of the massive table and explained how she liked the guests served. The test had begun. After offering her coffee, Julie served her an orange juice, and the fruit parfait. While Willow was delving into the parfait, Julie went back to the kitchen and dished up a serving of the quiche and the French toast, adding a twisted orange slice garnish for her presentation. Trying not to hover, Julie sat in a chair next to Willow and watched for her reaction. Julie didn't realize how much she needed approval.

"This is delicious! Not only will my guests remember it, they'll be asking for recipes," she said excitedly. "If you take the job, would you consider writing out and sharing your recipes? It would be another novel gift for our guests."

"Of course! That does sound like fun. Is it really that good?"

"When can you start work?"

"Really?" questioned Julie. The smile on Willow's face let her know that she had sealed the deal. "Let's see, as soon as I can get my rental turned in. Barbara said the closest place would be Salina. Then I guess I'm good to go."

"The bad part of the job will be that the inn is usually full on weekends. That's when I'll need you the most. I'd also want you to help with special events. But I can easily give you one free day during the week."

Julie didn't hesitate as she held out her hand to shake on the deal. "I just moved here. I don't have any set hours for anything. I would be happy to help with special events. As a matter of fact, it sounds like fun."

"Julie, I was planning on going to Salina for extra supplies this week. I could go tomorrow, and if you wanted to return your rental, you could ride back with me."

"Barbara Preston offered me a ride, but I think she was just being generous. If you don't mind, I'll take you up on that offer."

"Actually it would give us a good chance to talk about schedules and menus, and I can tell you about some of the plans I'm working on. Then if it's not too soon, I would love to have you start on Thursday, since we have a few guests booked. Does that sound okay?"

"It sounds good to me." Julie didn't want to appear too anxious, but it sounded more than okay to her.

Just then the front doorbell rang. Willow looked up and said, "I have guests arriving for this evening. I'll see you tomorrow after checkout time, say 11:30? Why don't you leave by the back door and check out the gardens?"

Willow headed for the front to attend to her guests. Julie went into the kitchen to get to the back door when she realized she couldn't leave just yet. The kitchen needed to be cleaned up first. After all, Maude had always taught her that a good cook always cleans up her messes.

~ 10 ~

Barbara was delighted when Julie gave her the good news. "We'll celebrate by having you here for dinner tonight," she said.

Julie was sitting at Barbara's kitchen table once again. Barbara was almost as excited as Julie. "But I should be taking you out for dinner," Julie said, "as a thank you."

"Honey, Shady Creek really doesn't have all that many places to celebrate in. From what you told me, you're going to be doing some experimenting with food. I volunteer to be an official taster." Barbara patted her ample waistline.

"Shady Creek really is a tiny little hamlet for someone like me who's never been out of big cities," Julie agreed. "It's charming, and the people are really friendly."

"I hope you feel like that forever, but I seriously doubt you will. You'll probably be bored silly eventually. We love it here though. We've always called Shady Creek our home, and to leave, someone would have to drag me out—kicking and screaming. Richard and I only have each other to take care of now—God willing we'll always be able to."

"Do you have children, Barbara?" Julie watched Barbara's demeanor change in an instant. Her eyes held the complexity of warmth and sadness, of strength and weakness. Quite unexpectedly they started to glisten with tears.

"Oh, Barbara, I'm sorry, I didn't mean to…"

"No, dear, you had no way of knowing," Barbara spoke in a heartbroken voice. "Yes, we had a daughter, and we think we have a grandchild." The energetic woman of a few seconds ago was gone. The new, saddened woman continued, "You'll find out about this if you stay in Shady Creek for any length of time. I think you should hear it from me, and there is no nice way of putting it. Over twenty years ago, our daughter Amanda, my sister Ruth, and her husband Don were all murdered." Barbara looked up at Julie and saw the horrified look on her face.

"Oh Barbara, I am so sorry," Julie felt terrible for asking. "You certainly don't have to tell me about it."

"Let me tell you so that you don't hear bits and pieces from someone else, since the house you rented from us is where Ruth and Don used to live before that day. They had just moved out of the house that you're living in because Ruth had MS and was in a wheelchair. She couldn't get around in a two-story home anymore, so they had moved to a nice little ranch house just over a couple of blocks from here. I still can't go by that house. I'll go ten blocks out of my way just to avoid it." Barbara's shoulders shook as she told the story now. Julie put her hand on Barbara's hand and squeezed.

"It's okay, Julie. I live with it every day. Sometimes it helps to remember; sometimes I can hardly bear it. But I want you to know the facts from me. When people in town find out where you're living they're bound to tell you some of the rumors that went with that night." Barbara took a deep breath and continued. "Anyway that horrible day started out so good. Jenny and I had baked some gingerbread cookies for Don and Ruth. Jenny was Amanda's little girl. Gingerbread cookies were Ruth's favorite. Jenny and I had so much fun baking those cookies. She was only two, but she was just the sweetest thing. She was so excited when Amanda told her they were going to take the cookies over to the new house. That was the last time we saw Amanda alive, and it was the last time we saw Jenny. Jenny just vanished. To this day, we aren't quite sure what happened to her. We pray that she was never harmed, but we just don't know." Barbara looked up, and Julie realized why her eyes showed such a longing. It was as though a deep cloud of pain covered her soul. Julie got up and got a box of tissues from the counter so that she and Barbara could use them. She put her arms around Barbara and held her tight. Neither woman noticed a silent Richard watching them from the doorway.

* * *

Walking home later that evening, Julie could think of little else but the incredible story Barbara had told her. It made her own problems seem so trite. Barbara had still insisted that they celebrate Julie's good fortune of landing a job at the inn. Since she and Willow's mother had been helping at the inn, she had lots of pointers and insights about what Willow's dreams were. Julie felt as if she could become part of the dream and was looking forward to the trip with Willow tomorrow. Of course that would leave her without transportation, but she would deal with that later.

Opening the front door, she was not disappointed to once again be greeted with the scent she had come to expect when she was in this house. No wonder she had been thinking of Maude so much. Maude made gingersnap cookies for her when she was little. She shook her head at the thought that the woman who lived here at one time loved gingerbread cookies too. It should have been disconcerting. It was not. As a matter of fact, it gave her a sense of well-being and belonging. She had even grown to like the occasional puffs of cool air that kissed her cheeks now and then when she walked through the house.

~ 11 ~

As she drove up to the front of the inn, Julie was glad she had decided to take Willow up on her offer of a ride back from Salina. She hadn't yet worked out the details of how she would get around once she got rid of the rental, but she knew she couldn't afford to have it one day longer. Seeing a guest's car still out front, Julie knew she would have to wait for Willow. She took the opportunity to observe the inn's architecture. Yesterday before her interview, she had not really noticed the secure, been-there-forever feelings given by the native yellow limestone structure.

Julie got out of the car and walked to the inviting porch that ran the length of the inn's façade. Willow had placed white wicker furniture in intimate groups here and there, and pots of purple and yellow pansies thrived in the cool shade of the overhang. The pansies smiling little faces had been strategically placed to welcome guests. Julie was about to take a seat in one of the wicker rockers to wait for her new employer when Willow appeared.

"Ready to go?" she asked.

Following Willow's car down the road, Julie was surprised at the diversity of the Kansas landscape. Just two short days ago, she had mostly been traveling on the busy interstate through a series of rolling hills. Large limestone signs had informed her that she was driving through a part of the Flint Hills of Kansas. Some of the hills had a soft fuzzy layer of spring green over them. Others still had tall red grasses waving in the wind. Twilight had just begun to settle on the day when she had taken Shady Creek's exit, and the hillside that nestled the town had greeted her with lights popping on here and there, reminding her of a huge Christmas tree.

Today Willow was leading her out of town on a less traveled highway. The road was winding its way around the large hill that held the town of Shady Creek. On the other side of the road was a creek lined with native elm and giant cottonwood trees. The creek and trees explained how the town had gotten its name.

As soon as they rounded the last curve, the hills disappeared and Julie realized she was driving on flatlands. She could see for miles as she drove almost parallel to the interstate highway some distance away on one side of the road. Fields of spring crops were between her and a tree-lined river on her other side. She relaxed and enjoyed the scene, knowing that soon she wouldn't have a car to take short drives in.

* * *

Willow drove to the airport in Salina and waited as Julie returned her rental. Julie let out a deep sigh, feeling an

enormous relief when she got into Willow's car. The girl at
the rental counter had looked at her suspiciously when she
said she wanted to pay for any additional charges with cash,
but Julie knew credit cards were a thing of her past for now.
All of her credit cards had been thrown in a trash receptacle
in Chicago after she had drawn out as much money as she
could on all of them. For someone used to living only with
credit cards, it had been a hard thing to do. But the colorful
character that had helped her get a new identification had
warned her to only use cash in all her dealings. Julie felt
like a fraud and cheat. She hated lies. It seemed as if the
past week she had been doing nothing but lying. She was
wondering if the lying part would ever be easy for her when
Willow interrupted her thoughts.

"Hungry?" Willow asked.

"Starved."

"Let's grab a quick lunch before I pick up the supplies.
Do you have anything you need to look for?"

Knowing that Willow had guests checking in later, she
just shook her head. She would deal with finding table
service some other time.

As the two sat eating a quick burger and drinking diet
sodas, Willow showed Julie her list of the food inventory
she liked to keep on hand for the inn. They talked menus
and recipes for a while. Julie was amazed at how passionate
Willow became when she talked about the inn.

"You love the place, don't you?"

"I've loved that house since I was a little girl. When
Daddy died he left Mom and me a fairly substantial
insurance benefit. The inn was up for sale the week after

we received the insurance money. It seemed like it was an omen. Mom was hesitant, but when she saw the gardens she couldn't wait to get her hands in the dirt. She and Barbara Preston have really done the gardens proud. And Richard actually built the gazebo for me. He's good people, Julie. If you need help in any way, don't hesitate to ask Richard. He loves to help others." Willow stopped for a moment to take a bite of her burger and then went on.

"He's also helped me with some of the maintenance on the house. I redecorated the guest rooms the way I wanted them, but thought I needed to remodel the kitchen. I'm hoping to do special events now that you're on board. I've had a lot of requests for that, but I realized real quick that I needed more help."

"I've never done anything like this before, but I get excited when I hear you talk about it. I hope my cooking doesn't disappoint you."

"You're from the city, right?"

"Uh huh," Julie said taking a drink and nodding. Stick something in your mouth, so you don't say too much, she inwardly advised herself.

"Well, did you go to many social outings yourself?"

"Oh, a few." Julie thought of all the times her mother had dragged her to her social events.

"Tell me what you remember most about them. I want people to come from other towns to Shady Creek, and I want a good word-of-mouth reputation. If we can make the inn something really special, I think it could be a go for more than a B&B. I want simple and economic foods, but want a good presentation, and of course everything needs to taste spectacular." Willow smiled and added, "Barbara and Mom will help us there with more recipes, and I know Richard will like the taste-testing part." She smiled every time she spoke of Richard, giving Julie the impression that he was indeed a very special person.

Oh, it was going to be hard not to let things slip out. Willow's enthusiasm was contagious. Julie had no idea getting a job could be this much fun, and she knew she was very capable of following a recipe. If Willow wanted her to experiment, it would be even more fun. "I think your ideas are right on target. I've stayed in a few very nice B&B's and I like your plans." She thought of all the things Stan complained about, in almost every place they had ever stayed. She wondered just what she had ever seen in that man.

Willow was gathering up her things. "We'd better get a move on. I have quite a few items to pick up today. Maybe tomorrow I can show you around the inn after the guests check out."

~ 12 ~

Julie awoke on Thursday morning before the birds had even thought about their morning chatter fest. She felt more independent than she ever had in her life. Today she was going to start a new job. It didn't sound like such an important job. Stan would ridicule her if he were here, but then, Stan wasn't here. She turned on the bedside lamp and took inventory of her room once again. When she had stopped by Barbara's on the way home from the inn, Barbara had given her a pair of crisply ironed, spring green curtains for the bedroom.

"Julie, I'm so sorry," she apologized. "I meant to have these put up in your bedroom before you came the other night, but I didn't have them hemmed yet."

Looking around the room, Julie couldn't believe how a pair of curtains could make such a difference. The yellow wallpaper roses had looked faded before. Now they looked misty. It was as though the curtains had worked magic in the room.

"Well HoHo, what do you think?" Julie asked the little wooden toy sitting on the dresser. "Stan would have a fit if he heard me talking to you too." She chuckled and headed for the shower. She was so ready to start her day.

* * *

Julie was working in the kitchen when she overheard compliments on several breakfast items. It had been a pure delight when earlier one of the female guests asked Julie how she had made "that French toast." Julie had already handwritten the recipe on several cards. When she gave the woman a card, the male half of the other couple asked for one too. The joke in their house was that he was the cook in the family.

As the couples lingered over conversation and several cups of coffee, Willow joined them and explained some of the inn's history. Julie cleaned up the kitchen and decided to explore the beautiful gardens in the backyard as she waited for the guests to check out. She could see Barbara and Rita's handiwork in the mixing of the flower and vegetable gardens. Iris in full bloom ran the entire side of one fence, explaining where all the fresh cut iris inside the inn had come from.

"Mom and Barbara have done a pretty darned good job out here," Willow said proudly as she joined Julie in the garden. She turned back toward the inn, announcing, "I've got time for that tour now." Julie followed as she headed for the screened-in porch on the side of the inn where patio tables and chairs were set up. Willow explained that this was where she hoped to hold dinner events in the warmer months. She opened a glass-paneled door that led into the parlor. It could just as easily have been called a library. A massive fireplace with built-in oak bookshelves took up all of one wall. The shelves were loaded with books and photos of the family who had built the house. Detailed contemporary carvings graced the wood on the fireplace mantel and tiny mosaic tiles made up the hearth.

"I've already had to turn down a request for a wedding in this room. I just wasn't ready for it at the time, but I think we could handle one now. Of course I need to coordinate events with guests staying here, but I think special events will bring in enough money to finally show a profit." Willow seemed to be working things out in her own mind while she explained everything to Julie. As they stepped through open pocket doors into the next room, Willow was describing it as "the hub of a wheel." The room accessed the parlor, the kitchen, the entrance foyer, and a sitting room. The only remaining space in the room was taken up by an enormous oak stairway leading to the guests' rooms on the second floor. Willow had placed an antique table in the middle of the room with a journal and pen, encouraging guests to leave a message. A quick glance told Julie that the guests who had taken time to write had warm memories of their stays.

Oak carved handrails on the open stairway led up five steps to a landing. There the stairs turned and continued to the second floor, with a banister on one side and a wall on the other. This was the "hub" of the second floor, called the Garden Room. Five separate bedrooms, each with a private bath, were on this floor.

"I put out fresh-baked cookies before check-in time for the guests up here," Willow said as she pointed to another antique table sitting in the middle of the Garden Room. An empty plate with only a few crumbs left testified that the guests had approved of the cookie plate. Books and magazines laid on several small tables. Several original art pieces hung on the walls. Willow explained that local artists shared their art in the hopes that a guest might want to purchase a piece. Cards beside each piece of art also listed the address of the small gallery and antique store down on First Street.

As Willow took Julie through each room, it was clear that she had put her personal touch on everything in the inn. The rooms each followed their own unique garden theme. The Daisy Room was light and whimsical, while the Sunflower Room took on more of a country feel. The Rose Room mixed deep shades of maroon and warm shades of pink. The Ivy Room looked like an outdoor arbor, and the last room was called the Iris Room, with a variety of blues and purples.

"Willow the whole inn is charming," Julie complimented. "No wonder you love it so much."

"I love showing it too, but I'd better get some work done now. It's good to have you on board, Julie. Oh by the way, we still haven't had you fill out the paperwork for your employment. I'm going to strip a couple of beds and pick up the linens while you go and do that. I put the papers on the desk in the sitting room. Let's get that done before you leave this morning."

Julie hoped the heat that was creeping into her face wasn't apparent to Willow. She knew the form would ask for things that she would need to lie about again. She turned quickly and grabbed the cookie plate on her way down the stairs.

When she found the paperwork lying on the desk, she sat down and stared for a long time, wishing she could use her real name and knowing she didn't dare. Picking up the pen and sighing heavily she began writing where the form asked for a name—Hendricks, Julie L.

~ 13 ~

Two weeks had already gone by with Julie working at the inn. Each day she could feel herself gaining a little more confidence in her own abilities. She was shocked to admit how much her self-image had been damaged by a man she had once loved. She walked a little taller now, and interacting with the guests at the inn made her feel her own self-worth. Humming a tune while she finished in the kitchen, she debated drinking the cup of lukewarm coffee she had poured herself earlier. Willow stuck her head in the kitchen and made up her mind for her.

"Hey, wanna grab a cup of coffee and join me out on the back porch?"

"Sounds good to me." Julie grabbed the cup and walked through the parlor and onto the porch where Willow had already sat down at one of the tables.

"I think I should rent a few folding chairs, just in case." Willow was talking more to herself than to Julie. When she realized what she was doing she looked at Julie sheepishly, "Sorry, I think out loud—a lot."

Julie smiled and nodded. She could never tell whether Willow wanted her input or if she was just talking through her own plans to answer her own questions. She took the last sip of her now cold coffee.

"What do you think? The Wellington party just called and said to plan on two more guests. Any more than that and I don't think it will work. Well, if the weather is nice, the overflow can go into the garden and gazebo—" She stopped talking for a minute and looked at Julie. "Here I go again. Can you tell I'm a little bit excited to launch this project? It's something I've always wanted to do—host parties. When I was a kid, I used to drive my mom nuts with tea parties in the backyard. I wanted to serve tea and crumpets; she wanted to dig in the dirt and plant flowers." She smiled a mile and continued, "And now we are both doing what we love."

"Sounds right to me," Julie said as she set her empty cup down.

"Julie, I want you to know that you're doing a wonderful job. I wouldn't be able to do this if I didn't think I could count on you—and of course Mom and Barbara. You interact so well with the guests in the mornings too. Several have told me how much they love getting your handwritten recipes."

"Thank you. I love meeting people. I love meeting the people of Shady Creek too. But…" Julie hesitated to find the right words, "Can I ask you something?"

"Ask away."

"Are the people in Shady Creek always so curious when a newcomer is in town? They certainly give me the once over when I see them, especially the older ones."

Willow's forehead furrowed as though she didn't know whether or not to ask, "Julie, has Barbara said anything to you about her daughter?"

"Yes." Julie hadn't spoken to Barbara about it since. She added, "What a tragedy!"

"It's not only that. You look so much like Amanda Preston that it kind of freaks people out. I know it did me. I still have nightmares about that night sometimes. Amanda and I were good friends. Even though I was an adult, Mom said she was afraid to let me out of her sight."

"I guess I just have one of those faces," Julie was starting to feel the familiar heat travel up her neck and into her face. "People have always told me I look like someone else they know." Willow just nodded and seemed to accept that explanation. But it was beginning to unnerve Julie just a bit, because no one had ever compared her looks to anyone else until she came to Shady Creek. The fact that the person she looked like had been murdered so long ago was just a bit creepy. "Did you want to talk to me about something else?"

"No. I just wanted to make sure that you know how much I appreciate your extra effort with the guests. Guess I'm nervous about the party too, my own expectations and all. Mom and Barbara both said they'll show up about an hour before the party to help serve. Are you sure you can handle all the food tomorrow afternoon?"

"If it's a problem, Barbara said to give her a call." Julie suddenly had a thought. "Oops! That reminds me—I said I would help her in the garden today, so before it gets any hotter I think I had better go—unless you need something else?"

"Nope, I think everything's good to go. See you in the morning."

Julie grabbed the two empty coffee cups and got up to leave, "Willow, thank you for giving me a chance." She walked back to the kitchen before she said anything more.

* * *

By the time Julie got to the Preston house, Barbara and Richard were both in the backyard working. They had been to the nursery and picked up young plants for the vegetable garden. Barbara was bent over putting a tomato plant in the freshly turned earth. Richard looked up from fighting with a soaker hose and smiled. "Hi there, kiddo. Want to grab that end and pull it through the other side for me? The durned thing got all tangled up when I put it on the shelf in the shed. I should just throw it out and go get another one, 'cause I think it has a few too many holes in it anyway. I'll check it out if I can ever get it untangled."

It was unusual to see Richard frustrated. Julie smiled, walked over to the hose, and tugged on an end to pull the hose straight. Richard just looked up with a feigned snarl and said, "Where were you ten minutes ago?"

Julie knew nothing about gardening. "What kind of plants are those?" she asked Barbara.

"I'm planting peppers and tomatoes today," Barbara answered as she slowly rose to her feet. "Rita and I exchange our crops when we harvest them. These are my favorite. She tries all kinds of vegetables. She's also got an herb garden every year. I don't usually have much luck with herbs so I just get them from her when I want them."

"Together those two women get enough produce to feed half the town," Richard laughed. "Hey, it could be worse. I could have fallen in love with a woman who liked to buy hats."

"Don't even ask him about that, Julie," piped up Barbara.

Julie smiled at them both. The good-natured banter between them always gave her a contented feeling. It must've been a blessing to have been together as long as they had and still be able to get along. It was so unlike her own parents' banter, which often turned into a hurtful silence. She wondered what Stan had told her parents when she disappeared. If her father was back from his latest overseas trip, he would want to call her.

"Julie," Barbara interrupted her thoughts. "Is everything ready for tomorrow? I'll bet Willow's excited."

"That's an understatement. I think it's mostly ready. Willow said I should take her van to pick up the rest of what I need this afternoon." She looked at Barbara and said, "You're going to have to show me everything about this gardening thing. My mother would never let me do anything that could possibly get dirt under my nails."

"Oh you poor thing," said Barbara with sincerity in her voice. "Here you go. You get to plant your first tomato plant." She handed the plant to Julie and showed her what to do. They all worked together for another half hour, Barbara patiently teaching Julie the tricks she had learned about gardening over the years. Julie was skeptical when Barbara showed her how to cut a plastic straw and slip it around the stem of a pepper plant. Barbara said it would keep the grubs from destroying the tender plant while it established its roots. Julie didn't even know what a grub was.

They were bent over the plants when suddenly both women were assaulted by a rush of black-and-white fur.

"Blaze!" came a scolding deep voice behind them. But Blaze totally ignored the rebuke and started giving Barbara kisses with a sloppy, wet tongue. Barbara giggled like a schoolgirl and hugged the happy dog.

"Oh Blaze, I've missed you." She held on to the dog for a second longer and then said, "Okay, you can go see Richard now." The border collie rushed over to Richard to greet him in the same manner.

"Dan, when did you get back?" asked Barbara as she wrapped her arms around the beautiful man who seemed to belong to the dog.

"Got back late last night and slept in late this morning."

"Julie, come meet Dan," Barbara said as Dan held out his hand. Julie brushed her hands on her pants to wipe off as much dirt as she could. When she turned so that Dan could see her face, Julie missed the look of surprise in his golden brown eyes that were hidden behind dark glasses. She had no idea that he was looking at her with the same expression that the rest of the townspeople had when they met her. But Barbara caught the reaction.

"Dan, Julie is our new tenant. We know she looks a lot like our Amanda," Barbara explained casually.

"The likeness is remarkable. It's like looking at Amanda's photo. Excuse my manners," Dan said, somewhat embarrassed. "Very pleased to meet you, Julie."

"Pleased to meet you too, Dan," she said as Blaze came over for her introduction.

The dog stood by Dan's side and wagged a greeting while Dan introduced her to Julie. She then walked toward Julie, waiting patiently for a pat on the head.

"Well, you do have some manners after all," remarked Richard.

Julie scratched behind Blaze's ears, making the dog a friend for life, while Barbara described Dan as Will Barclay's grandson. "Will and his wife Helen are our dearest friends— and of course Dan and Blaze too." Barbara went on to say that Dan and Blaze had been gone for a couple of weeks on vacation visiting one of Dan's college buddies.

"I talked to Ray the other day. He'll be glad you're back. Said he's getting too old to do his job all by himself." Richard turned to Julie to explain, "Ray is Dan's deputy. Dan's our county sheriff now. Will was the sheriff in Shady Creek back when dirt was invented. He finally retired and got his grandson to follow in his footsteps." He added proudly, "He does a mighty fine job of it too."

Barbara looked over at Julie and saw how red her face was, "Julie, you've been out in the sun a little too long; you're getting awfully red." Julie was thankful the extra sun was hiding what she was feeling. All the lies she had been living the last couple weeks made her feel like a criminal. And Barbara and Richard were good friends with a sheriff!

As they walked toward the house, Barbara was asking Dan, "How are Will and Helen doing? I haven't seen them for a while."

Julie didn't pay much attention as Dan was reporting on his grandparents' health. She didn't hear Dan telling Barbara, "We're a little worried about Granddad Will. Something's not right, but I think Grams finally talked him into seeing Doc Jensen."

While the others went into the house, Julie excused herself to go home, saying she needed to get cleaned up so that she could pick up things for the party. As the others talked over their concern for Will Barclay, she had no idea his welfare would soon have an impact on her life.

~ 14 ~

On the outside Will Barclay still looked like the typical county sheriff. He had a small paunch, but still had the strut and the overpowering look of someone a person wouldn't necessarily want to mess with. However his insides felt the true story. Deep inside his gut he held a dark secret of guilt.

When Will had finally retired from his position as sheriff, his grandson, Daniel, had immediately filled his boots. Even though Dan was only twenty-two at the time, he had won his first election easily. He had studied hard on his criminal justice courses in college and knew a lot of things about peacekeeping that Will didn't know. But he had learned most of what he knew about taking care of Shady Creek from following his grandfather around since he'd been a little tyke. Will was proud of the job that Dan was doing.

But soon Will Barkley would no longer be around to advise his grandson. Will sat in a stage of disbelief. Somehow all the past years of his life as Shady Creek's sheriff had not prepared him for the sentence he had just received. Dr. Mark Jensen's words lingered in the air a long time before they drifted in to settle on the comprehending part of his brain.

"Will, you've neglected yourself too long on this one. I wish you had come to me sooner, but the tests show you're in the final stages. We can be really aggressive and give you treatments, but the odds don't look so good." He hesitated a few seconds before he added, "I can recommend several good doctors…"

Will shook his head and held up his hand to stop Mark's words. He and Mark Jensen had been friends for a long time. They had had differences, but each respected the other. Neither ever pulled any punches with the other, so Will knew Mark would be straight with him when he finally said, "You know, Doc, all these years as the sheriff, I was always prepared for you to take out a bullet or something a little more dramatic. But I guess death doesn't always give you the choice. How long do you think I have to play around here on this earth?"

Mark smiled at his friend, "You know I can't answer that one." When he saw Will get that argumentative look on his face, he continued, "But I will tell you to prepare Helen and Dan." He spoke slowly and with compassion, "I am saying that you need to get your house in order. And don't wait too long."

Will rose from his chair slowly. He suddenly felt much older than his sixty-eight years. He held out his hand to his friend. "Thanks for giving it to me straight, and thanks for putting up with me all these years."

Mark grabbed Will's hand, and in a show of friendship and sorrow he pulled Will close for the kind of hug that two macho guys rarely give each other. Neither spoke another word before Will left the office. Both knew that Will wouldn't want treatments if he couldn't win the battle.

Will Barclay got into his car and started driving around the town he had lived in all of his life. He cared deeply for almost all of the people in the town, even a few he'd arrested a time or two. When he drove past the cemetery, he was thinking that he would be buried there soon. He stopped his car and sat and stared at the three graves that held his guilt that was almost unbearable. He had spent the last twenty-two years covering his pain. Now that he would be facing his maker soon, he knew he couldn't carry all of that guilt to his own grave. He knew he wouldn't ever be able to face the Prestons, but he had to let them know about their granddaughter.

By the time he left the peaceful cemetery, he knew what he had to do. On the drive home he prepared himself to talk to Helen. She had put up with a lot over the years. Now he was going to ask her to tell no one that he was dying. He had no idea what he would tell Dan.

* * *

Dan had lived with his grandparents since he was four years old. He knew something was wrong the minute he came into the house. Grams looked as though she had been crying and Granddad Will held a look that he couldn't quite read.

"What's wrong?" he asked as he looked from one to the other. Neither answered him. They shot looks between them and both looked away. Blaze quietly went to Will, who was seated at the kitchen table, and put her head on his lap. She drooped her tail with only a hint of a wag. Will's big hand dug into her fur feeling the warmth of the dog.

"Okay," Dan paused, "let me try this again. What the hell happened?"

"Will, you may not want me to talk to anyone else, but Dan is not anyone else!" Helen said defiantly. Will's shoulders slumped even further, if that was possible. He quit rubbing Blaze and wiped over his face with his hand.

"Dan, sit down. We have to talk."

Helen and Will sat with Dan at the kitchen table and talked and cried together as only a family can. Blaze lay quietly on the floor beside Will, occasionally sitting up to put her head on his lap. Will was adamant that he wanted no one except those in the room to know that he was dying. Dan said he knew that Richard and Barbara would want to know. He was surprised at the reaction he got from his granddad. He was vehemently against telling his best friends, and when both Dan and Helen questioned him as to why, he simply said he had his reasons.

Helen shook her head, not understanding. "They're our best friends. They'll never forgive me for not telling them. Besides how on earth are Dan and I supposed to keep this from them? They'll never understand."

But Will insisted. He promised, "I'll write them a letter, explaining my reasons, but no one will know until I'm gone.

I don't want to talk about this anymore. That's the way it's gonna be!"

For a few minutes no one said a word at the table. Will got up and started into the next room. Blaze followed him. Dan sat with Helen. "Grams, do you know anything about this?"

But Helen only shook her head. "I don't know what he's thinking." Her shoulders started to shake. "I know that he's carrying some kind of guilt around with him when it comes to the Prestons. He's never told me, but I think it's because he never found Amanda's murderer."

Dan knew that the triple murder that happened so long ago haunted his granddad. He had observed how upset Will had become when the state tried to close the case. He never quite understood any of it, but he chalked it up to the fact that he was just too close to all those involved.

Dan reached across the table and gave his grandmother's hand a squeeze. "We'll get through this okay, Grams," he said with the voice of a child. He knew how stubborn his granddad could be.

~ 15 ~

Dan was running hard and paying little attention to the dog running with him, but Blaze was sticking close, sensing something wasn't right.

When Dan had been introduced to Blaze, it was love at first sight—for both of them. So it was a given that as soon as Blaze was old enough to go on Dan's morning runs, the dog was seen by his side. A few times when she was still mostly pup, Dan had run a little too far. He then had to carry the pooped-out puppy back to his house in his arms. As Blaze grew, her stamina grew. Now she would run ahead of Dan, sniffing out all kinds of interesting things. Then she would wait patiently for him to catch up with her, only to bound off to explore more bushes and scents. But this morning Blaze stayed by her master's side.

Dan finally slowed enough to let deep thoughts into his brain. It had been several days since Granddad Will had dropped his bombshell. Now Dan was worried about Grams, and he was worried about his granddad too.

Yesterday he realized he was downright pissed off at the man he had loved and admired for as long as he could remember. How could he just accept a death sentence and give up? And why in the hell would he not tell his best friends? Dan was damned tired of making excuses when the Prestons asked about Will. He didn't want to have to lie to them. The man who had been Dan's father figure since he was so young had secluded himself in his home office. Why was he shutting Dan and Grams out of his last days?

So yesterday Dan had gone to Doc Jensen, hoping to get some answers. Doc hadn't been much help.

"Dan, I know how much you love your granddad, but you have to let him work this out in his own way." Doc sighed and continued, "Fighting him won't help, and to be brutally honest with you, I don't think he has enough time left to spend it fighting."

"I have to think of Grams too."

"Son, I've known that stubborn old man for a long time. You aren't going to change his mind about telling his friends good-bye. He is fighting some kind of demon—has been for a long time. I don't know what it is, but just let him know how much you love him." Doc then showed Dan to the door. Dan had been dismissed.

Dan knew Doc was right, but he didn't have to like it. He had gone back to work and not been able to concentrate. And last night he had tossed and turned. He was losing his Granddad Will. He wanted to help him and didn't know how. He could accept his granddad's death; he knew he had no choice. But he felt like the man was rejecting him and it hurt like hell.

* * *

While Dan was out running with Blaze, trying to figure out why Will Barclay was cutting himself off from the world he would soon be leaving, Will was cleansing his soul. He had sat up all night trying to compose a letter to right a wrong he had committed. He knew the task was futile. He could never take back his actions the night Jenny Preston had disappeared. But he could not go to his grave with the knowledge that Jenny was alive the last time he'd seen her, and he had let no one know. He prayed that the letter he had written to the Prestons would not bring them more pain. God only knew they'd had their share and then some. But he knew in his heart that they should know the truth. He also knew they would hate him—that was why he couldn't tell them any other way.

He looked up at his computer monitor, reread the three letters he had written, hit PRINT, and took a deep sigh as the printer transferred his words to paper. He put each letter in its own envelope. He wrote on one: *To: Helen and Dan— Open only when I'm gone*. He wrote on the other: *To: Richard and Barbara—Please forgive me*. He wrote on the last letter: *To: Danny—only to be opened after the Prestons have read their letter*. He went back to his computer and highlighted the letters. He then hit delete.

Will put the letters in the top drawer of his desk, turned out the light, and went upstairs to his bedroom. Helen was just waking up as he climbed into their bed.

"Helen, I think I can sleep for a while now," he whispered. As most of the town was just waking up, Will closed his eyes and slept peacefully for the first time in a long, long time.

* * *

Dan slowed his pace. The run had helped. He decided he would try to approach Granddad Will again and let him know how much he loved him—the man who had raised him. He would not be cut off from the old man's last days. Feeling much calmer and determined, he turned and started in the direction of home. He had run farther than his usual run so he took Maple Street home. He had just passed the Shady Inn when he saw Julie Hendricks walking to work on the other side of the street. She looked as though she was carrying a heavy burden on her lovely shoulders. He had seen that look before when he was on the job. If he hadn't been so concerned about his granddad, he might have recognized it.

~ 16 ~

Things had been going so smoothly for Julie since she had escaped to Shady Creek that she was unexpectedly flustered this morning. She was awakened in the wee hours by a dream. It was haunting enough that she had not been able to get back to sleep. The images of the dream kept floating past her so that she finally got out of bed to start her day. But even her morning shower had not erased the faces of the two children in the dream. They were the same children she had seen in reality at a truck stop that first day of her new life as Julie Hendricks.

She thought back to that day. The children were dirty and unkempt. The woman with them was battered and bruised. They all looked scared and lonely. When the children asked their mother if they could get a hamburger, she tried to shush them. Julie saw her counting out the bills for gas and suspected that she didn't have enough money for both. Julie knew how scared she had been that very morning when she had packed her bags, even though she had been planning her escape for quite some time. She knew nothing about this woman, but she knew scared. She had tasted it the first time Stan hit her. She had seen it enough when she looked in the mirror. She wasn't sure she had enough to share, but she approached the woman and pushed several bills into her hands anyway. Then she walked away and didn't look back.

She had not thought about those children or the woman again until she'd had the dream this morning. In the dream the children were clinging to their mother, but their mother kept pushing them away toward Julie. Instead of helping them Julie started running in the other direction. Soon Stan was running after all of them. Julie was running toward her mother, but Katherine turned and ran from her. Her father was standing in the distance. And that was where she woke up. The dream played over and over in her mind.

By the time Julie was finally headed to the inn, she had come to the conclusion that the dream was a sign—she was homesick for her father and mother. Would they even know she was gone? Ever since she had been married, it wasn't unusual for her and her mother not to talk for a week or two at a time. Since her father traveled so much, she talked to him even less. But her father should've been back in the States by now. Maybe she should try to call him today. Then she thought of Stan. She shuddered when she thought about the look in his eyes the day she had finally gotten the courage to leave. As she got to the back door of the inn, she wondered if she had been honest enough with her mother. Maybe she should have gone back to Katherine and shown what Stan had physically done to her. Once again her mind flashed images of those children. She wondered if they and their mother were safe.

She said a little prayer for them and a prayer of thanks for herself. She entered the inn and welcomed the job she held there.

* * *

The inn was at full capacity. Julie soon got busy enough to push the dream from her thoughts. The nine guests she had just served breakfast lingered over their morning coffee, all sitting together at the large dining table. They were talking about places of interest they hoped to see on their travels through Kansas. Julie gathered dishes and asked if anyone wanted more coffee. She was in the kitchen when she heard Willow greet the guests in the dining room.

"Good morning everyone. I hope you all had a good night," she said. Everyone agreed that they had a good night. Several comments were made about the comforts of the inn. Willow started to give her usual "tour" speech when one elderly gentleman spoke up.

"Willow Johnson," he said. "Could you be any relation to Pete Johnson?"

Julie heard Willow pause. "He's my ex-father-in-law. Do you know Pete?"

"I did a long time ago. Let's see, Beatrice, how long has it been since we lived in Shady Creek?"

"We moved about four years after those horrible murders," answered the man's wife. "So I guess we've been gone for eighteen or nineteen years."

Several people around the table spoke at once, "Murders? What murders?"

"When we lived here, oh, I think it was about twenty-one or twenty-two years ago, there were three murders in town one night and a little girl disappeared. It was the talk of the town." The man paused for thought. "Did they ever find out who murdered that…who was it…uh the Shepmans?" he asked Willow.

"And what about that little girl? Did they ever find out what happened to her?" asked Beatrice.

"No," Willow's voice took on a strange tone. Julie heard Willow suddenly excuse herself and leave the room.

Julie felt prickles run down her spine as the same puff of air that she often felt kissing her cheek at her house suddenly was here at the inn. She stopped what she was doing so that she could hear the conversation better. Now that the couple had the attention of all, they were going into vivid detail about the murders. It seems that they had lived two blocks away from where the murders occurred. Every time either of them mentioned the little girl, Julie could see the children's faces of her morning dream. She felt an unfamiliar sensation, like she needed to hide. She didn't want to hear the couple's stories, but she couldn't stop listening. She could taste something salty: tears running down her cheeks to the corner of her mouth. She needed air. Suddenly what the couple was saying was something she couldn't bear to hear. She went out the back door and didn't stop until she found herself sitting on the porch swing in the quiet gazebo. What was wrong with her? What had just happened? Barbara had told her about the murders and she hadn't felt like this. Closing her eyes she set the swing in motion and let the rhythm calm her.

"Are you okay dear?"

Julie looked up to see Willow's mother, Rita McGee, looking at her oddly. Julie had been so distraught when she came outside that she hadn't even seen the woman in the straw hat bent over the herb garden. Climbing the two steps up into the gazebo, Rita stood by the swing until Julie scooted over and patted the seat. Julie had met Rita when she and Barbara had helped with two very successful special events at the inn. She liked Rita as much as she liked Barbara. She was a spark of liveliness, and no one around her ever had to guess where she was coming from. Richard called her a straight shooter.

"You didn't look so good when I stood up. You nearly scared the devil himself out of me."

"I'm sorry, Rita. I guess I'm just having a really bad morning."

"Something happen in the inn?"

"No, not really…well, yes…maybe," Julie said, not knowing what had upset her so much.

Rita gave her a questioning look, "That explains it then." Both women laughed lightly.

"A couple in the inn—an older couple—they said they used to live in Shady Creek. They were asking Willow if they had ever caught the Shepman murderers. Of course then the other guests started asking questions and so they were telling them all the gruesome details. I don't know why it affected me the way it did." Julie stopped talking for a minute and then continued, "I guess maybe it's just because I've become so fond of Barbara." She looked over at Rita who was now looking away from her so that she couldn't see her face. Trying to explain she began again, "Barbara told me that her daughter was murdered and all…I just don't know why I got so upset this morning." There were a full two minutes of silence before Rita spoke.

"Barbara and I were very good friends back when Willow and Amanda went to school together. Everyone in this town was touched in one way or another. We're a small community; we pretty much know almost everybody. Everybody talked about it, but after the funerals not many would talk 'with' Barbara. I suppose people just didn't know what to say. I know Will and Helen Barclay did, but everyone else just talked behind her back. They said some mean things about Amanda too. Some people even said if she hadn't gotten pregnant that they would all be alive yet." Rita looked at Julie and shook her head. "Nobody knew that! They never did find out why she was killed. I figured it could have been anybody in town. I was afraid to let Willow out of my sight."

"I know, she told me that."

"I don't know. I got to thinking how I would have felt if it would've been my daughter that had been killed. I don't have any grandkids, but I couldn't even imagine having a little one like Jenny and not knowing what had happened to her." Rita paused and then went on, "I went over to Barbara's one day when she was having an especially hard time. She poured her heart out—the good feelings and the bad. I've learned to just listen when those bad days creep up on her."

"Doesn't it hurt her to talk about it though?"

"The murders? Yes. But she needs to talk about Amanda and Jenny. They were part of her, and she doesn't ever want to forget them. It was her sister, Ruth, and her husband Don too. Oh she lost so much that day."

"What can I say to her, to help her?"

"Julie, has she shown you any pictures of Amanda?"

"No," Julie paused, "but she did say I look a lot like her. Willow told me the same thing. Rita, the last thing I want to do is hurt Barbara."

Rita was nodding. "You could ask to see a picture of them. She's proud to show pictures. She hasn't shown you because she didn't want you to think your likeness to Amanda was the only reason she's so fond of you. Barbara simply likes you, girl. That's just Barbara." The two sat together for a few more minutes, letting the quiet of the garden soak in.

"Thank you for telling me all of this, Rita," Julie said as she put her arms around the woman and hugged her. "I think I'd better get inside and get that kitchen cleaned up now, or your daughter will think I ran out on her."

"And I saw a few weeds earlier that have my name on them."

Both women went back to their own tasks—Rita with a definite purpose and Julie with a much lighter heart.

~ 17 ~

Dan was still in uniform when he stopped by his grandparents' home mid-afternoon. He knew how proud his granddad was of his position. Maybe that pride would make him more approachable. He hated confrontations with either of his grandparents. Even when he was in high school and had gone through a period of rebellion against some of their rules, he had hated the confrontations. Maybe it was because some of the kids were intimidated by Will as sheriff. Maybe it was because he had also seen the vulnerable side of Will. The real reason was probably because he loved the man so much. After his morning run with Blaze, he had decided to go against Doc's advice and try to get to the bottom of what ailed Will Barclay.

While most of the houses in Shady Creek had their air conditioners going full blast during a Kansas summer afternoon, Grams wasn't fond of air conditioning. So the front door was open. He reached for the screen door and heard laughter coming from the kitchen. He hadn't heard laughter in this house since he had come back from his vacation—since Will had told Dan and his grandmother that he was dying. He walked on in, standing in the house and relishing the sound. When he went on into the kitchen he couldn't believe his eyes. Grams and Granddad were sitting at the table holding hands and still chuckling. Dan looked at his granddad and saw how normal he looked. How could he be dying? He also saw something in the man that he hadn't seen before—something in his expression that Dan couldn't read. Clearing his throat, he let them know he was standing there watching them.

Will looked up and smiled, "Hi, son, come on in."

"How is everything going?" he asked cautiously.

"It's good. We've got some news to share."

"You're going to be okay?" the words coming before Dan could think.

"Well, no, not quite that good," Will shook his head. "But your grandma and I have a surprise. We're going on a vacation together before I get too sick to travel."

"But…"

Will held up his hand to stop any protests from Dan. "Your grandma and I never had a decent honeymoon, Dan," he said quite solemnly. "I called Doc and got his okay, well, maybe I should say I let him know our plans. Son, I'm taking this woman to Hawaii. I want to do this for the woman who put up with me all these years."

Dan looked from his grandmother to his granddad. Grams looked radiant. Clearly Granddad Will was pleased with himself. Something had changed. Dan didn't care what it was—he was just going to be thankful.

"Are you sure you're up to it? Granddad Will? Grams?" concern came through Dan's voice.

Each of them looked at Dan, saying nothing, nodding in the affirmative.

* * *

By the next day, Dan was picking up his grandparents to take them on the three-and-a-half-hour drive to the Kansas City International Airport. His granddad must have made all the travel arrangements during the last several days when he was isolated in "his" room that he called his home office. Under any other circumstances, Dan would have been thrilled to see his grandparents go on a much-deserved vacation together. Now he was just confused. Granddad Will looked good. Maybe he had lost a little of his color, but he looked better than he had for years.

While Grams was busy running through the house making sure the iron was unplugged, and the plants had all been watered, Will quietly motioned for Dan to follow him into his office.

"In case something happens, son, I need to know that you'll do something for me."

"Sure, Granddad. Just tell me what it is." Dan noticed that familiar weight on his grandfather's shoulders again.

"There are letters in my top desk drawer. Here's the key. One of the letters is to you and your grandmother, and the other is for Richard and Barbara. I can't leave until I have your promise that when I meet my maker, you'll read your letter." Will looked at his grandson with a pleading that

Dan had never seen in him before. He looked old right now, having a hard time asking Dan for this favor. Dan reached out for Will, but his granddad brushed his arm away and grabbed Dan by both shoulders. "This is really important, Daniel. It'll explain a few things to you. I want you to take the letter to Richard and Barbara and be with them when they read it. You'll understand then. Please say you'll do that for me?"

"Of course I will, Granddad." Dan knew how hard it was for Will Barclay to ask anyone for anything. Doc Jensen's words popped into his mind just then. "And Granddad, I want you to know how much I love you."

"I love you too, son, and I'm proud of what you've become. I know I don't have to say this, but when I'm gone…" Will started to choke up, "Just take care of your grandma for me."

Will handed Dan the key and grabbed his grandson in his arms in an embrace like he hadn't given him since he was a kid. He had so much strength in those arms. Dan remembered how safe they had made him feel when he had been a scared little boy. Oh how he didn't want his granddad to die.

* * *

As Dan drove back home from the airport, he reflected on the happiness he had just left. It seemed surreal that his grandparents had acted like a couple of love-struck teenagers on the way to the airport. Helen had been more excited than Dan had seen her in a long time. She wasn't a huge talker, but today she hadn't stopped talking from the time they left until they got to the airport. Once they had arrived, Dan had helped them with their tickets and bags. As they approached their security check, he hugged his grandma good-bye. She had tears welling in her eyes. Will just winked at him, seemingly content to have made his wife so happy. When he hugged his granddad and said good-bye, he got the lecture he had heard since he was a kid.

"Not good-bye yet, just so long," Will said with a touch of sadness in his voice. "We'll see you in a couple of weeks."

"Oh my! Everything has been happening so fast that I forgot to call Barbara and tell her where we're going." Grams said. "I can't believe I didn't call her. Dan, will you stop by and tell her? Oh, I'm just so excited."

"Grams, just enjoy. Have a good time. I love you. I'll tell them," he had promised as they moved through the line and away from him.

The drive back to Shady Creek was relaxing for Dan. He smiled to himself, taking his time and enjoying the beauty of the Flint Hills on I-70. He loved the view from the crest of the hills. The setting sun on the Kansas landscape gave him a kaleidoscope of colors that were constantly changing. He felt like he was on the top of the world. It had been such a good day. He thought perhaps Doc Jensen could be wrong. Maybe the tests were wrong.

As he turned off the interstate, he remembered his promise to Grams. Right now he needed to get home to let Blaze out. He would wait until tomorrow to talk to Barbara.

~ 18 ~

Dan didn't get to deliver Gram's message to Barbara until late the next morning. On duty he parked his patrol car in front of the Preston house and walked around to the backyard. He figured they would still be working in their gardens before the day got too hot. Sure enough he saw Richard, Barbara, and Julie Hendricks huddled together like a football team, planning their next play. Richard handed something to Julie.

"Go ahead," Richard urged. "Take a taste."

Julie took the red ripe tomato from Richard and bit down. Juice squirted out, followed by a stream running down her chin. Richard was waiting for a reaction.

"Oh yum!" Julie closed her eyes and added, "I had no idea a tomato could taste this luscious." She held the rest of the tomato out to Barbara, and Barbara took her share. Richard finished it up.

"That, my dear, makes all this hard work worth the effort," Barbara said with satisfaction.

"First tomato of the season?" queried Dan with a grin on his face. All three pairs of eyes turned his direction.

"You're too late my boy. The first one's gone," laughed Richard. "But it served all three of us. Looks like soon we'll have more tomatoes than we'll know what to do with."

Dan looked over at Julie. She didn't look like the same woman he'd been introduced to earlier in the summer. She looked relaxed and was clearly enjoying herself. He noticed a tomato seed stuck on the end of her chin. Her hair was wet with sweat, and wispy bangs were plastered to her forehead. It was apparent that she had been digging in the dirt with Barbara, but she had a different demeanor about herself, and when she looked at him and smiled, Dan's heart did a little flip. She was beautiful—tomato seeds and all.

"Did you bring Blaze?" she asked.

"No, I'm on duty," he looked down at his uniform. "I've got the patrol car, and I can't stay."

"Well, we haven't seen much of you lately," complained Barbara.

"I had a lot to do when I got back, to catch up and all," he hoped he sounded convincing. "I didn't realize the summer was going so fast." The fact was he had been avoiding the Prestons, therefore avoiding the questions about his grandparents.

"And how about Will and Helen? They're sure keeping themselves scarce. It's about time Will and I get some fishing in before the summer's all used up," said Richard.

"Well, that's why I stopped by. Grams wanted me to tell you where they are right now." Both Richard and Barbara had a question behind the look they gave him as he continued. "Granddad Will surprised Grams—and me too. They took off for Hawaii yesterday."

"Hawaii!" Together Richard and Barbara expressed their surprise.

"Granddad said he wanted to give Grams the honeymoon she never got. Let me tell you, they were both acting like a couple of lovesick teenagers when I took them to the airport yesterday."

"Well, I'll be!" Richard said shaking his head. "I would never have thought Helen could get Will to take a trip any farther than Kansas City." Richard was chuckling, but it was clear that he really didn't believe it. Dan said no more for fear that he would give away something about his granddad's health. Instead he started asking questions about the garden produce. He had done what Grams asked and told Barbara about the trip. Now he knew he should leave. But he was enjoying being with Richard and Barbara, and he wanted to enjoy the view just a bit longer—even though the view had wiped the seed off her chin and replaced it with a smudge of dirt.

"I really do need to get back to work. Ray has been doing a lot of covering for me lately." Dan looked toward the house, as if he was going to leave.

"Dan, will you come for dinner tonight?" Barbara asked out of the blue. "Julie and I have a new recipe we want to try on you guys." Julie had no idea what Barbara was talking about. As far as she knew she was going home and having a sandwich for dinner.

"Uh, sure. I'd like that," Dan smiled. "Regular time?"

Barbara nodded. "And make sure you bring your other half," she winked at Julie. A little embarrassed by Barbara's remark, Dan turned and walked back to the house.

"See you later," he called over his shoulder. He smiled to himself when he got in the patrol car. "Nothing subtle about you, Barbara," he said under his breath as he headed back to work.

* * *

Using the baking sun as an excuse, Richard took off for the house. Julie was questioning Barbara with her eyes.

"We'll be in too, just as soon as I pick a fresh bouquet for tonight." Barbara started toward her flower garden with Julie on her heels.

"Just what recipe are we trying for tonight?" Julie asked. When Barbara didn't answer Julie pinned her down. "Barbara, I recognize a set-up when I see one. It's been a long time since I've had a matchmaker get me a date." Of course Barbara had no idea that Julie was a married woman. She also couldn't know that Julie didn't want to get involved with anyone just yet. She didn't know that Julie had to get her own head on straight before she could think about getting involved with another man. Oblivious to these things, Barbara was quite pleased with herself. She picked a rather large handful of flowers and handed them to Julie.

"Julie, Dan is family to me. It's just dinner," she chose her words carefully. Knowing she hadn't convinced Julie, she added sheepishly. "Okay so maybe I was hoping. And we did want to try out that new chicken dish on Richard." Barbara couldn't seem to erase the smile that had planted itself on her face. "I would really like to see you and Dan get to know each other. He's such a nice boy...well...man. And he doesn't have many serious female friends. And he's not hard on the eyes."

Julie looked down at her dirty clothes. She felt sweaty and grimy. Barbara was right. A little over six feet, dark wavy hair, and a man in a uniform—he was a good-looking man. Surprised that the uniform didn't bother her anymore, Julie looked at Barbara and shook her head. "I guess a girl can never have too many friends." She shrugged her shoulders and added, "And you're right, he's not too hard on the eyes."

* * *

Everything seemed to focus around the kitchen table in Richard and Barbara's house and tonight was no exception. Julie had gone home and showered, walked to the grocery store, and picked up a few items to make a surprise for dessert. Now the women were busy in the kitchen working together.

"We'll eat in the kitchen tonight," Barbara explained as she started setting the table. "You know, we should eat in the dinning room once in a while, but Dan has always said my kitchen is his favorite room in my house. I haven't seen much of him lately. I learned a long time ago not to take any relationship for granted," she took a deep breath. "Julie," she continued, "I want to show you something. Can you come with me for a minute?"

Julie followed her into the dinning room. It was a lovely room, but Julie realized she had never been in it before. Barbara had a buffet along one wall with family pictures hanging above it. Reaching up and removing one of the pictures on the wall she handed it to Julie. Julie was shocked when she looked at the photo up close. It could have been a picture of her!

"This was Amanda, wasn't it," she spoke almost reverently. Barbara nodded.

"And this one," Barbara turned and took down another framed photo, "was Amanda and Jenny together."

"This explains a few of the reactions I've received around town," Julie said as Barbara nodded again.

"Maybe it's why I've felt so comfortable around you. I hope it doesn't make you uncomfortable around us—that I show these to you. I don't want you to think that I am trying to make you into my daughter."

Julie searched deeply for the right words, "Barbara, I had a long talk with Rita the other day. She told me how you and she are such good friends." She stopped for a moment, looking at the photo again. "It's uncanny that I look so much like your daughter. I know I haven't told you much about my background. I would like to tell you more—about why I came to Shady Creek. And I want you to be able to talk to me about Amanda too. You must have precious memories in your heart. If you want to talk about them, the good times and the bad, I want to be a good enough friend to listen." She stopped and looked from the photo to the mother of the girl in the photo. Her eyes were moist, but she had a smile on her face.

"Thank you," was all Barbara said as she put her arms around Julie and gave her a hug. They were interrupted by the timer on the oven. Barbara hung the pictures back on the wall as Julie went into the kitchen to check on dinner. The now familiar puff of cool air was here too, kissing her as though it was giving her a message.

~ 19 ~

The fragrance of honeysuckle drifted onto the porch, where the party of four had moved after dinner. Barbara and Julie had tried out a new recipe. While edible, it had received a disappointing review from everyone except Dan.

"Hey, it's sure better than any chicken I've fixed lately."

Julie was glad she had made the whipped peanut butter dessert that was also on trial. Everyone agreed that it was a big hit. She had saved enough to take Willow a sample in the morning. If Willow approved the dessert, she would offer to use it for one of the special events at the inn.

Dan was sitting on the top step of the porch stairs leaning against a railing, while Julie sat on the other side of the step. Blaze was lying between the two with her head in Julie's lap, taking advantage of the gentle massage she was getting behind her ears. A faint creak from the porch swing that Richard and Barbara shared caused Blaze to occasionally lift one of her ears. It didn't seem to pique her curiosity enough to move any other part of her body. A cicada interrupted the otherwise quiet evening.

Julie looked at Dan and asked, "Why Blaze?"

"Excuse me?"

"Why did you name her Blaze?" She heard Richard chuckle softly in the background. "Is it because of the white streak in her face?"

"Her name is actually Blaze II," explained Dan. Blaze raised her head and turned slightly when she heard Dan mention her name. She quickly dropped her head back into Julie's lap for more petting.

"You still didn't tell her why you name your dogs Blaze," chuckled Richard.

"Okay, but you have to promise not to laugh," he waited until Julie nodded. "When I was about ten, I started asking Granddad Will for a horse."

"Hounded him would be a better description," added Richard.

"I saw an old movie with the most beautiful horse I'd ever seen. She had this huge white star in the middle of her forehead. Her name was Blaze. My dream was to have a horse like Blaze. I thought I could keep her in the garage and let her eat the grass off the front lawn. I couldn't see a problem with that—Granddad could. So I suppose I did hound him a little. Anyway he finally told me that I could get a puppy instead. We went to Salina and picked one out of the pound. She had the white stripe on her face. It wasn't a star. But the minute she licked my face, I fell in love with her. That was the first Blaze." Blaze picked her head up again and looked at Dan when she heard her name. He reached over and patted her reassuringly.

"When I lost her, I was devastated. And then I found Blaze II." This mention brought a little wag of the tail. "She's just a pup yet. Her manners need a little work, but we'll get there." There was a moment's pause in the conversation before Dan asked Julie, "So did you have a pet when you were growing up?"

"Not really."

"Where did you grow up, by the way?"

Julie hesitated for only a second before she answered, "The city—nothing with a quiet yard and a back porch swing."

"Is the city Kansas City or New York City?" Dan quizzed.

"My, the mosquitoes are starting to bite. Is anyone for going in the house?" said Barbara.

"Thanks, Barbara, but I really need to go home," Julie was thankful that Barbara had broken the line of questions she was afraid Dan would ask. "Thanks for the evening, and I'm sorry about the chicken."

"That peanut butter fluff thingy you made more than makes up for the chicken," said Richard.

"Hey, I still liked the chicken," added Dan.

"Peanut butter fluff," Julie smiled, "I kind of like that as a name for it."

Dan slowly stood and stretched his legs. "I need to be going too. How about if Blaze and I walk you home, Julie?"

"Sounds good. Hey, Blaze, time to wake up." Julie gently nudged the dog, who looked like she was perfectly content to sleep on the porch all night as long as Julie kept stroking her.

* * *

Julie's house was only four houses away. It was much too short a walk for Dan. He really wanted to get to know Julie a little better, but he wasn't sure she felt the same. He got the feeling that she didn't want to talk about her past at all. As a matter of fact, she hadn't talked about her past all evening. Everything she talked about was her life in Shady Creek. Of course he'd been dodging any talk of his grandparents all evening too. He noticed Barbara giving him a strange look a couple of times. She had always been able to see through him, even before Grams had. Well it wasn't his choice to keep his Granddad's illness a secret.

"We're here," Julie's voice broke the silence. "It was really good to get to know you Dan. Barbara and Richard think the world of you and Blaze and your grandparents."

"Yeah, they're good friends," Dan said. Julie had unlocked her door and was waiting for him to leave.

"Well, good night." Looking at Blaze, he said, "Come on, girl, we'd better go home too." Blaze turned to Julie for one more pat before she started walking with Dan.

"Good night, you two," Julie said as they headed down the sidewalk.

Julie let herself in and went directly upstairs. As she headed for the bedroom, she heard a soft tapping sound. Cautiously she reached around the corner and flipped on the light switch. HoHo was gently rocking back and forth. But the minute she stepped into the room, the little rocking horse stopped. Julie stared at her beloved toy, disbelieving. "Okay, I'm not imagining this. What the heck is going on?" She sat down on the bed and stared at the toy. Nothing moved. There was no rocking. Two button eyes stared back at her. Trying to convince herself that she was in control of all her senses, she gave the freaky little horse an ultimatum.

"Okay, HoHo. No more games. Be good or you're going in a drawer."

She went in the bathroom and brushed her teeth. Still standing in the bathroom, she peeked her head around the corner of the door to see if HoHo was rocking again. The toy had not moved. She shook her head. "Okay, Julie, get a grip!" She got into bed and kept looking at the horse. She had just had such a wonderful peaceful evening. But now she was disturbed by a toy she had loved since she could remember.

* * *

When Julie woke up the next morning, the bedside lamp was still on. She chastised herself for being afraid of ...what? The dark? It was an easy thing to do now that daylight was starting to work its way into the room. Now she couldn't even figure out what it was that had spooked her so. Her memories were of a pleasant evening spent with friends. It was so different from anything she had grown up with.

She thought she could trust the new friends she had made the last several months. But then she'd thought she could trust Stan at one time too. Had he always had a mean streak, or had she done something to make him that way? She hadn't doubted herself for a while now. Was she strong enough yet to go back and face her past life? Would her father stand behind her, or would he tell her she needed to grow up, like her mother had? She wondered what Stan had told her parents. She really needed someone to help her sort out her feelings. But who? If she told her new friends, would they turn on her because she had lied about who she really was? Whatever she decided it would have to wait because she had a job to get to. She would just have to wait a bit longer to confide in anyone or to call anyone in her past. Jennifer Kingman's friends, and even her family, would probably find Julie Hendricks rather boring. Julie thought that was ironic, because she was beginning to really like the new her.

* * *

Dan Barclay was sitting at his desk in the sheriff's office thinking about the emotional roller coaster he had been on the last several weeks. He had come back from his ski trip refreshed and relaxed. Then he had walked into the news that his granddad was dying. He was ready to tear his hair out when his granddad had secluded himself, but then Granddad Will did an about-face and took Grams on a honeymoon. Doc Jensen had made it sound like Granddad Will was going to croak any minute, but he sure didn't look sick when he had left him at the airport. Then last night—it was nice. He loved Richard and Barbara as much as he loved his own grandparents. And Julie Hendricks had stirred feelings in him that he hadn't had for a female since Rachel Ann McCormick had dumped him in high school. He looked over at Jolene, his dispatcher/secretary, and asked, "Hey, Jolene, whatever happened to Rachel Ann McCormick?"

"Three kids, divorced, living in Arkansas I think," she answered. "Why? Thinking of rekindling a relationship?"

"No way; just wondering."

Dan tried to get back to the stack of papers he had piled on his desk, but pleasant thoughts of Julie kept interrupting. When the phone rang, Jolene answered it on the first ring.

"It's Tom, down at the convenience store—looks like he had some vandal damage again last night."

Relieved to have an excuse to get out of the office Dan picked up his hat and started for the door. "Tell him I'll be right there."

~ 20 ~

When Dan realized that Julie walked to work every morning at about the same time he went running with Blaze, he changed his route to include Maple Street. The Shady Inn just happened to be on Maple Street, therefore dog and man got to see Julie on her way to the inn every day. Blaze, bless her little heart, always wanted to cross the street to say hi to Julie. Dan would follow her and pretend to apologize. While Blaze was rewarded with a quick pat on the head, Dan usually received a dynamite smile. It made the extra blocks well worth the effort. Then at the same time Julie got to the inn, he and Blaze would take off for the running path out by the old highway.

He usually stopped at his grandparents' house on his way back from his runs to bring in the morning paper and the mail from the day before. It had already been almost two weeks since they had left on their vacation, and it still felt strange to go to their house every day and not have either one of them there.

Dan had only gotten two phone calls from his grandparents since they'd landed in Hawaii. The first time he talked to both of them, but the call last night was only from Grams. When he asked how Granddad Will was doing, she hesitated just a bit too long before she answered.

"Fine, we're both fine. Will's just a little tired though. We'll see you tomorrow, Dan." She had a heaviness in her voice and disconnected quickly when she was sure Dan had the correct flight number and arrival time at the Kansas City airport.

As soon as he told the Prestons that his grandparents were coming home, Barbara started planning. She wanted a homecoming dinner waiting for them when they got back to Shady Creek. Dan had tried to talk her out of it, but she had insisted.

"Dan, I haven't seen Will and Helen in forever and a day. And besides, I want to hear all about their trip. They have to eat somewhere. They'll be tired, but they can go home as soon as dinner is over. I'll understand." Dan was hoping Grams and Granddad would understand.

* * *

When Dan got to the airport, he went directly to the baggage claim where he had told Grams he would meet them. They were taking a while to get there. He recognized their bags, so he grabbed them and stood waiting for his grandparents. Finally he saw them walking toward him, but if he had not see Grams first, he wouldn't have recognized his grandfather. He was walking, but very, very slowly. He looked as though he had lost at least twenty pounds, and his salt-and-pepper hair was now almost white. He turned away from them so they couldn't read the shocked expression on his face. When he was eleven, he remembered being punched in the gut so hard that it had knocked the wind out of him. That's how he felt at this very minute. How could his granddad's condition have changed so quickly? Taking a deep breath and trying to compose himself, he turned back around and waved at them.

Approaching, he noticed that they both looked happier than they had in a long time. Gram's arms were open as he went into them.

"I know it doesn't look so good, Dan," she whispered. "It's okay though." She smiled and stepped back so that Dan and Will could hug. Dan couldn't imagine how anything was okay. He grabbed his granddad and managed to say, "Welcome home. I've missed you guys."

Once they were finally on the road, Grams talked nonstop while Granddad Will napped in the backseat. Dan couldn't remember his grandmother ever acting this way before. It was apparent that the trip had been good for her. But he knew he was not hiding his concern about his granddad. He was thankful that he didn't have to say much.

About an hour away from Shady Creek, he told Grams that Barbara had dinner waiting for them. He wasn't sure what kind of reaction that would get, but Grams was delighted.

"Are you sure Granddad is up for it?" he asked as quietly as he could.

"Granddad can handle dinner just fine," came a groggy voice from the backseat. "Besides I may not get many more chances, son."

Dan looked at his granddad in the rearview mirror but couldn't read his face. Grams was looking away from him, suddenly watching the scenery flash by as they traveled down the interstate. When she finally looked back at Dan, there was a sadness there that had been covered up before. Dan wanted to ask more about his granddad's health but thought better of it. All of them were silent for a while.

* * *

Julie had made a raspberry cheesecake as her contribution for the dinner at Barbara and Richard's house. She arrived early at the front door and knocked.

"Land sakes, girl, how many times do I hafta tell you, that you don't hafta knock. Just come on in," Richard said as he opened the door for her.

"I come from Ch—uh, the city, Richard. I just can't get used to that."

Barbara was busy in the kitchen, so Julie went in to help. The two worked well together. Richard was watching the evening news in the front room. When the two women finished dinner preparations, they decided to go sit on the back porch with a glass of tea.

"Richard, we're going out back," Barbara yelled into the other room. They sat together on the porch swing as Barbara talked about Will, Helen, and Dan. Julie had decided earlier in the week that she was going to confide her real identity to Barbara. She thought she was finally strong enough to get her past life settled. But tonight was a night to meet Dan's family, and she wouldn't spoil Barbara's fun by talking about her own problems.

"I can't believe you've been here for a couple of months and still not met Helen and Will," Barbara said. "They—"

Richard interrupted Barbara with, "Hey girls, the gang's all here."

* * *

When Richard saw Dan's car pull into the drive, he went out back to get Barbara before they went to greet their friends at the front door.

"Oh Lordy, what's wrong with Will?" gasped Barbara under her breath the minute she saw him. But Helen was out of the car and running up the walk for hugs and introductions. She stopped short when she saw Julie standing a little behind Richard.

"Oh, and you must be Julie!" Helen said. She was shaking her head, as though to clear her thoughts. She looked back at Dan, who was helping Will get out of the car. Just then Will Barclay looked up at his wife and the woman she was talking to. He turned white as a sheet. Both Dan and Richard reached out to catch him as he stumbled backward.

"Will, my God! Are you okay?" questioned Richard. When he followed his friend's gaze he realized immediately why Will looked like he had seen a ghost. He had grown so used to Julie the last couple of months that he didn't think about other people's reaction to how much Julie looked like Amanda. Dan must not have said anything to his grandparents about the likeness. But it didn't explain why Will looked so thin and why he looked as though he was twenty years older than the last time Richard had seen him. Will was still staring at Julie with his mouth agape.

"Will, this is Julie Hendricks, our new tenant," explained Richard.

"But...but...," Will slowly turned his puzzled face to look at Richard.

"Yeah, I know. She's a ringer for our Amanda."

Julie could feel her face reddening. She had gotten used to the double takes when she met new people, but she had been in town long enough that almost everyone knew her by now. And then it hit her. This was the man who had found Amanda Preston and the Shepmans after they had been murdered. She had seen her own likeness in the pictures Barbara had shown her, so naturally he would be taken aback. But more than shock was going on here. Dan's and Helen's faces showed concern for Will. Barbara's reaction when she saw Will getting out of the car was odd. And Richard was at his friend's side in a heartbeat. What could she say to ease this situation?

"Hi, Mr. Barclay. I'm so glad to finally meet you," Julie said as she stepped forward to shake Will's hand.

"Well, I'll be a monkey's uncle," Will replied as he looked into Julie's eyes.

* * *

The rest of the evening was filled with stories of Hawaii and memories of times the friends had spent together. Julie caught Will looking at her several times out of the corner of her eye. When she would catch him, he would quickly look away. He also winced, as though he was in pain, several times. She was sitting beside Dan and she could feel him tense whenever it happened, so she knew something was not right. Richard had asked his friend how he could go to Hawaii and lose weight with all the luaus. There was chiding that Richard was just jealous that he couldn't get rid of his own paunch. But it did not go unnoticed from anyone at the table that Will ate very little. Julie could see the concern on everyone's faces.

Dan and Julie insisted on clearing the table and cleaning the kitchen while the others went to the back porch to talk. When they finished Julie stepped onto the porch too and said good-bye for the evening. The inn was full tonight, and she would have a big breakfast to prepare early in the morning. Dan offered to walk her home again, but she declined. She knew he was anxious to get home to let Blaze out, as a neighbor had been taking care of her for the day. Richard was pumping Will to give him a day for that fishing trip he wanted. Everything seemed so normal and relaxed. But when Richard and Barbara said their good nights to the Barclays as they got into Dan's car, Will hugged his friends in a rare embrace and told each of them good-bye. Dan could hardly say good-bye because he had a lump in his throat and could feel hot tears behind his eyes. He was glad the evening sky was darkening. He knew what his granddad's good-bye meant. His granddad always said so-long, he never said good-bye.

~ 21 ~

Julie's morning had been busy, which she always enjoyed. She was getting more and more comfortable interacting with the guests at the inn. A week ago Willow had even taken a rare night off and left Julie in charge because there had been only two couples registered. It had been an easy night, and all had gone smoothly. But what it did for Julie's self-esteem was astounding. She knew that if Willow had faith in her, she was doing a good job. The two women were becoming friends too. But Julie didn't want to compromise that friendship with her past. She also wasn't sure what ramifications her false identification could have for her employer. She had made up her mind to confide in Barbara today. Now that she felt safe from Stan, she thought it was time to get that part of her life cleaned up. And even though she knew Barbara would keep no secrets from Richard, she preferred to talk to Barbara alone. If Richard was home, she would ask for some girl time.

After Julie left the inn, she went directly to the Preston house. She stepped into the backyard, but Barbara was not in her gardens, instead she was just sitting on the back porch. As Julie approached, Barbara looked up. She didn't look so good.

"Good morning, dear. I've had enough of the garden today."

"Good morning yourself. Barbara, are you feeling okay?"

"Not really," she answered. But when she saw Julie's uneasy look she explained, "Oh I just didn't get much sleep last night. Richard and I talked quite a while. We're both a little worried about Will. He looked awful."

"I'm sorry, Barbara. Do you think meeting me had anything to do with that?" Julie just didn't know what else to say.

"Oh no, dear. You *were* a little bit of a shock. But he's lost so much weight, and his hair! His hair wasn't white a month ago. I know he had some color in his face, but good grief, he was just in Hawaii. Don't you think he would be a little more tanned?"

"He did look like he didn't feel too well."

"I think he was in pain too. I saw him grab his side a couple of times. And he loves my pot roast, but he didn't eat hardly anything!" Barbara stopped talking for a few seconds. Julie had no idea how to make Barbara feel better. She offered to go inside and get them both some tea. When she came back out, Barbara started back in as though Julie had never left. "And another thing, Richard is worried too. Richard thinks Will is really sick. He made a big deal about Will saying good-bye last night." Julie's brows knit together, trying to figure that one out. When Barbara looked at her she relaxed and chuckled. "Oh it's a superstition, that you never say good-bye, only so long. He would never let Dan tell us good-bye. It always had to be so long. Good-bye means forever." Barbara paused for a minute before saying, "Julie, I think he was telling us something. I think he might be very ill. That trip, out of the blue, was not the Will we know."

"I'm so sorry, Barbara. I don't know what to say."

"Thanks for listening dear. That helps more than you know." Barbara looked up at the sun, "Gracious, it must be noon already. Richard is having lunch at the café with a friend. Will you stay and have lunch with me? I couldn't eat breakfast this morning, and I am starting to get a growl in my tummy."

* * *

During lunch Julie mostly listened, as Barbara seemed to need to talk. Barbara told her about her and Richard's friendship with the Barclays again. She also talked about how Will and Helen had lost their son and daughter-in-law in a horrible accident.

"Of course they were able to have Dan in their grief," added Barbara. "Thank the Lord he had been with his grandparents that night and wasn't in the car with his parents." Barbara stopped for a moment and then apologized. "I'm sorry for the mood I'm in today. Most days I can stay on top of things but not if I don't get a good night's sleep."

"Barbara, any time you want to talk, please feel free to talk to me. I can't imagine what it was like—losing your family like that."

"Richard and I have always been each other's foundation. I think that's what has gotten us through the last forty-plus years together. But there was a time when Richard couldn't talk to me and I couldn't talk to him. I hardly remember any of the funerals. I was numb. But that first year I felt like I had a red-hot poker stuck through the middle of my heart. We searched and prayed that somehow Jenny would come back to us, but the not knowing was unbearable. I think I was almost to my breaking point. I was so filled up with anger and hatred that I thought I was going to explode. Doc Jensen told me that if I didn't get rid of some of my stress I was going to kill myself. He also told me how Richard was terribly worried about me. But we couldn't talk with each other anymore."

Barbara took a deep breath, and Julie realized her friend's wound would probably never heal. "I just cannot imagine," was all she could manage to say again. What words could help now?

Barbara continued as tears filled the corners of her eyes. "I have never told anyone this Julie—not even Richard or Rita. I started walking. Doc said that would help with some of the stress. I sometimes walked for hours. Amanda used to like to walk too, but I never had before that time. Anyway have you ever been over to Shady Creek's park?"

Julie nodded.

"It was in the fall. There was so much of God's beauty in the nature around me. I went to the butterfly garden in the park. The town made it as a small memorial for Amanda, Jenny, Ruth and Don. There's a little polished granite bench with their names etched on it. I sat down on the bench and begged God for some kind of understanding. It was late enough in the fall that it was way past the time that butterflies should still be around, but three of them showed up and landed on the butterfly bush next to the bench. Maybe I was desperate, but it was as if it were a message directly from the heavens." Barbara looked into Julie's eyes hoping she would understand.

"I think I can identify with that somehow." Julie didn't know why, but she associated what Barbara had just said to a little wooden rocking horse that seemed to be sending her messages.

"I have no idea how long I sat and watched those three beautiful creatures. There were only three. I willed there to be four, but there were only three. And when they flew away they all took off at the same time. At that very moment I felt a great burden lift off of me. I no longer felt the rage that had been burning inside of me."

"Did you finally get some kind of understanding?"

"Well, it was the understanding that I had to let go of the hate. It was killing me and doing no one any good. And then I also had a hope. There were only three butterflies—not four. Somehow those butterflies represented Amanda, Ruth, and Don—but not Jenny. It gave me hope that Jenny lived that night. She didn't join the others." She looked at Julie and asked, "Do you think I'm crazy for thinking that?"

"It's exactly what I was thinking when you told me the story."

"I think some people would think I've lost my marbles if I told them that. I haven't ever been able to share those feelings with anyone—not even Richard. But after that day

I think I started to mend enough that Richard didn't have to worry so much about me. We started to share some of our emotions again. We even laughed sometimes."

* * *

It was midday before Julie left Barbara's. As she was walking home, she realized that she had dodged her own confession again. She always felt like her problems were miniscule when she thought about the problems Barbara had dealt with over the last twenty-plus years. No, she couldn't have put another problem on Barbara's shoulders today. But she was also sure that Barbara was the one she would tell about Stan. Then maybe she would be able to call her parents.

Julie said a prayer of thanks that she had found a friend like Barbara on her journey to her independence. Barbara was worried about her friends today, so Julie would wait just a bit longer to confide in her. She remembered how Dan had looked at dinner a couple of times last night and knew that he was worried about his granddad too. She came to the realization that she was worried about all of them. She had been lonely for a long time and hadn't felt like she had any friends. It was good to have friends once again. It was good to have someone else to care and worry about.

~ 22 ~

Dan could hardly find the energy to put one foot in front of the other on his morning run. He didn't go past the inn as he had for the last several weeks, and he no sooner got to the running path than he was ready to quit. He called a disappointed Blaze back to him and headed home. Blaze was reluctant. Dan had been gone the whole day before, and she missed their routine jaunt. Then he came back to her and didn't want to let her run free. The dog was keen to her master's mood, and she knew something was wrong.

Taking his grandparents home last night, Dan knew for sure that Granddad Will was not going to be with this world much longer. As soon as they had stepped into the house, Helen dug into her purse and pulled a prescription bottle out. Will headed to the kitchen for a glass of water to wash a couple of the pills down. With Granddad out of earshot, Grams had explained, "Dan, Doc gave him something that is letting him live out his last days relatively pain free. The kindest thing we can do for your grandfather is to be with him and love him while he's still here. It's time to enjoy every second we can." She said it in such a firm voice that it was almost a scolding. Then she thanked him for picking them up at the airport and told him to go home. The end—she said no more. He had gone home and cried like a baby. Today he hardly had the stamina to get out of bed. It was going to be a long day.

* * *

Dan was curt to Jolene several times before she finally had enough.

"Excuse me!" came out a little strong from the normally friendly voice. "Did I do something to piss you off or what?"

Dan's shoulders slumped, and he sighed. "I'm really sorry, Jo. I've got a personal problem, and I don't mean to take it out on you. Maybe if you gave me a lead on who the little snots are that vandalized Tom's store, I could go hassle them for a while."

"Yeah, well, I'm going to call and warn my friends not to break any laws today." She laughed quietly and then looked over at the guy who was usually so mild mannered. "Seriously Dan, is there anything I can do?"

Dan shook his head. If he opened up to anyone, he was afraid of what he would say.

* * *

Julie knew she shouldn't wrap herself up in her new friend's problems, but she couldn't get Dan's sad look from the previous night out of her brain. She had not met Dan and Blaze on her way to work this morning and, coupled with what Barbara had told her, she thought Dan might need an ear too. She had no idea what time he normally got home and she had never seen where he lived, but she thought Barbara had said it was on Birch. She decided to explore the neighborhood a little and started walking toward Birch Street.

Sure enough, down the block she saw the sheriff's patrol car sitting in front of one of the houses. Julie walked up to the front door and knocked. She heard Blaze's familiar bark. A surprised Dan opened the door as Blaze bounded out the front to greet her.

"Hi, you two. I didn't see you guys this morning on my way to work. I wanted to make sure you were okay."

"Hi yourself. Got time to come in?"

"Sure." Julie wasn't exactly sure why she was here. "I was out exploring the neighborhood, saw the car, and figured this was your place."

Dan got the little grin on his face that Julie loved to look at. She thought many girls had probably been taken in by that grin. But behind the grin was the same sadness she had witnessed the night before when he was with his grandparents. She didn't want to tell him about her conversation with Barbara, so she played coy instead.

"How 'bout a soda? You can relieve me from ear scratching duties for a while to earn it."

"Sounds good. How about that, Blaze? Want your ears scratched?" she asked the dog, who was already nudging her hand for more pats.

Julie was surprised to see plastic coverings over furniture that was mostly in the middle of the room when she entered Dan's house.

"You'll have to excuse the mess. I bought this house about a year ago. It's time I got around to fixing it up a little. I'm in the process of painting. Well I guess that's not true. I'm in the process of getting this room ready to paint. How are you with a paintbrush?"

"An artist's paintbrush I can handle, but anything bigger I've never tried."

"Oh, it's so much fun. I could teach you how."

"You don't really look too convincing when you say that."

"I'm actually hoping it will be fun. I don't know what I'm doing either. Granddad Will was going to help me, but now…" Dan just shook his head and headed for the kitchen to get them both something to drink. Julie followed with Blaze at her side, who nudged her with her nose every time she quit petting.

"Dan is everything okay? Barbara mentioned that your granddad looked awfully thin." Dan was quiet for some time. He turned around and faced Julie as he spoke slowly.

"No, Julie. Things aren't real good right now. But for some reason Granddad doesn't want anyone to know." He handed Julie her drink and took a sip from his own. "I know Richard and Barbara were shocked at how he looked last night. I was too yesterday when I went to the airport. Just two weeks ago when they left for Hawaii, Granddad looked fine. I really had hoped that maybe he wasn't as sick as he said he was. Then when I picked them up yesterday, I was totally stunned." When Dan looked at Julie this time she saw not only sadness, but fear. And then the expression changed. "Shit! I shouldn't be telling you this. Please don't say anything to anyone—especially Barbara or Richard." Blaze, as if on cue, left Julie's side and went over to Dan.

"Oh, Dan, I'm so sorry. Of course not, if that's what you want." Just then the phone rang. When Dan started talking it was obvious that his grandmother was on the other end of the line. "Blaze, would you like to go outside?" Julie said to the dog as cheerfully as she could. She tactfully went out the back door, Blaze by her side.

Dan joined them in just a few minutes. By then Julie had found one of Blaze's balls lying around, and she and the dog were in a hot game of fetch. Dan joined them for a few minutes, looking even sadder than he had before.

"You can't wear her out with this game," he warned.

"I think I've figured that out," Julie said as she threw the ball again. "Everything okay? Dan just shook his head and looked away for long time before he said anything. He took a deep breath and turned back toward Julie.

"How about a beer and a pizza?" he asked. "I need to just have some fun for a while before I go over there."

"That's the best offer I've had all day." Julie smiled softly. It had been a long time since she had been asked out for a pizza and a beer. She thought back to a time when she was in college and she and Stan had gone out with friends for pizza. It seemed like a lifetime ago.

~ 23 ~

After the beer and pizza, Dan dropped Julie off at her house and then went on to his grandparents. Julie had been the medicine he'd needed. They had laughed and joked and kept things light. She wanted to know all about his life, but when he had asked about hers she gave pretty evasive answers. Something wasn't quite right about it, but he wasn't sure what. Was he just suspicious of everyone because both his formal education and his grandfather had trained him to be that way? He couldn't worry about it now.

Grams met Dan at the front door. "Your grandfather is in his office. Something has him agitated again, but he won't tell me what it is. He wants to talk to you though. It might have something to do with your job, Dan. Heck, I don't know. He was so relaxed the last couple of weeks that I didn't think he would go there again."

Dan hugged his grandmother and then put both his hands on her shoulders and held her at arms length. He looked deep into her eyes and tried to reassure her, "It'll be okay, Grams. I'll talk to him." As he went down the hall to the back room, he was once again grateful that Julie had brightened his mood.

"Hi, Granddad." Dan went over to his granddad and sat beside him. "Grams said you wanted to talk to me."

"You bet I do." Will Barclay looked at his grandson. Always one to get to the point quickly, he blurted out a question, "How well do you know Julie Hendricks?" There was a warning tone in Granddad's voice that Dan didn't like.

"Why do you want to know about Julie Hendricks?" Dan asked cautiously. When his granddad just kept looking at him with *that* look, he finally answered. "She just popped up out of nowhere. I guess I don't know much about her. She's from the city."

"What city?"

"I don't know. Look, Granddad, I've had a few other things on my mind besides some innocent girl who is trying to get her life together..." Dan stopped short. He hadn't even realized what his instincts had been telling him about Julie. "I guess I really don't know anything about her at all," he finally admitted.

"I wasn't thinking all that clear last night. Those pills I got from Doc are wonderful to keep me going, but I don't think so straight when I take them. But I do know that when I saw that girl last night I thought I was looking at Amanda Preston—Helen and I both did. I just think it's mighty peculiar that someone that looked so much like Amanda would be at the Preston house." Will Barclay's shoulders sagged. He shook his head to try to clear his thoughts. He raked his fingers through his white hair. "Son, it's always been my feeling that Amanda's little girl lived. And when I saw that young lady last night—maybe I just want to think that she would show up some day." He looked at Dan "I don't know—maybe it's just the pills I'm on. Daniel, it's my fault that little girl was never found."

"Granddad, how can you say that?" Dan was perplexed. "I've read that case so many times when you've pulled out the file. If the state guys couldn't ever find her, how in the hell did you expect to? You were too close to the family. You can't blame those murders on yourself."

Will knew that his grandson would soon know the truth about the night that still haunted him, but he didn't have the guts to tell him to his face. It would have to wait until he was gone. "Just remember to listen careful. People will tell you what you should think of them if you just listen careful."

"I will, Granddad." Dan realized that he had just listened carefully to what had been said by his granddad, and what he had heard was sending him conflicting messages. Will got up and went over to his recliner. For now the conversation was over.

"Close the door on your way out, son," Will said as he lowered his thin frame into his favorite chair.

* * *

Grams was sitting at the kitchen table drinking a cup of chamomile tea. "Did you get him calmed down?" she asked Dan when he came into the room.

"Grams, he still feels responsible for those murders that happened over twenty years ago, doesn't he?"

"Always has. Things like that change a person, Dan. It was especially hard since he had lost his own son, your daddy, only two years before."

"I guess I always thought of that as my loss, since it was my dad and mom. I didn't think of it as a loss for you and Granddad."

"Honey, you were only a little tyke. Of course you didn't."

"Okay then, let me think of you now. How are you Grams?"

"I'm doing okay. But I'm really tired. Is he in the recliner?"

Dan nodded, "I think he'll fall asleep. I'll go too, Grams, and I'll see you tomorrow."

Dan got up and kissed his grandmother good night. On the short drive home, he thought over what his granddad had said about Julie. Just to give the old man some peace of mind, tomorrow he would do some checking into Julie Hendricks's background.

* * *

Helen Barclay finished her tea and went into the office to tell Will she was going to bed. But Will was sleeping so soundly in his recliner that she got a blanket out of the hall closet, put it over her husband, and turned out the light without waking him. Then she went on to bed.

When Helen got out of bed the next morning, she wondered why she didn't smell the coffee she usually awoke to. Will was always up earlier than she was. She always prepared the coffeemaker the night before, and he would turn it on as soon as he walked into the kitchen. If he was too ill to make the coffee, she knew something was wrong.

She was not surprised when she found him, still in his favorite recliner—his fight already over. She calmly went into the kitchen, turned on the coffeemaker, and called Dan. Then she sat at the kitchen table with her head in her hands and wept for loss of the man she had loved the better part of her life.

~ 24 ~

Richard and Barbara Preston had offered to stay with Helen and Dan for a bit longer, but Dan told them they would be fine. He and his grandmother had a mound of sympathy cards to go through, and they needed some time alone for that task. The funeral was over, Will was buried, and now life must go on for everyone else. Doc Jensen had told Helen and Dan that it appeared Will's heart just quit. And even though they knew that Will would have wanted his death that way, they still had not been prepared. But they both knew others who had lingered, and they were grateful they had not seen Will waste away that way.

Dan had felt numb for the last three days. The town of Shady Creek had been wonderful, and he had been told many stories of his granddad's heroics as the county sheriff. A few of Dan's old high school friends who had since moved on to other places in life came back to mourn with Dan and his grandmother. One even recollected that if it had not been for Sheriff Will straightening him out, he never would have gone on to become the man he was now. Those were the stories that helped Dan the most. There were other stories that hadn't ended with a love for the sheriff, necessarily, but told of a better respect for the law itself.

"I wish Will could've known how some of these people really felt about him," Helen said.

"Grams, I didn't know that he had helped so many of my friends. Guess at the time some of those things happened I was acting kind of like a turd myself."

"Your granddad always said that a kid had to have a little rebellion in him. He said many times that without a little spunk, a kid wouldn't grow up to be much of anything."

"Did I have enough?" Dan smiled at Grams. "Spunk, that is?"

Helen gave a genuine laugh and nodded thoughtfully. "You certainly did," she finally answered. She grabbed another card. "I need to put a few of these aside and reply to some of them with letters." She started a new pile. But when Dan heard his grandmother say the word letters, it rang a bell.

"Grams, that reminds me. Granddad left a couple of letters when you went on vacation. He said he had a letter for me and one for the Prestons. I didn't think about it until just now. Do you have any idea what they're about?"

"He told me he'd done that. I don't know why, because he wouldn't tell me anything else about them. But he said you would talk to me after you talked to Richard and Barbara." Helen sighed heavily and continued, "Dan, I don't know what to expect from those letters, but they were important to him."

"I guess I need to see for myself," Dan said as he got up. "I have the key to his desk at home. You be okay while I run home to get it?"

"I'll be fine. I'll read a few more cards while you're gone."

* * *

When Dan came back to his grandmother's house, he had Blaze with him. As soon as she was in the house, she ran into Will's office. When she didn't find him there, she ran into the kitchen with Helen. Dan poked his head in the kitchen too and said hi again before he headed back to his granddad's office. He didn't ever remember being in this room before unless his granddad was in it. It was such a strange sensation. If he hadn't promised Granddad Will that he would take care of this last request, he didn't think he would've been able to come into this room just yet.

Opening the desk drawer he saw the letters immediately. To his surprise there were three letters lying in the drawer instead of two. The first was addressed *To: Helen and Dan— Open only when I'm gone.* The next was addressed *To: Richard and Barbara—Please forgive me.* The last letter was addressed to Dan alone with instructions underlined. Dan read—*To Danny—only to be opened after the Prestons have read their letter.* Dan could not imagine what any of this was about. Why would his granddad be asking the Prestons to forgive him? He opened the first letter and began to read. It was addressed to both him and his grandmother, but the letter inside was only to him. His hands were shaking as he read.

Dear Dan,

First I want to tell you how much I love you. Your Grams and I were devastated when we lost your mom and dad. But raising you was the blessing that came out of that tragedy. I am so proud of you that I could bust!

Dan, I am going to ask you to be with Richard and Barbara when you give them their letter. They love you almost as much as Grams and I do, and this confession will affect all of you. None of you are going to like what I have to say, but I have to give you the facts. Try to forgive me for what you learn in that letter.

The second letter for you will explain just a little more after you hear what I have to say to Richard and Barbara.

I know you will look after your grandmother when I am gone. She knows nothing of what I am about to reveal. I have been the one with the secret. She has been true in your life.

I love you, Danny

Dan read the letter three times before he looked up and realized that Grams was standing in the doorway looking at him.

"Are you okay, Dan?" she said with deep concern in her voice. Blaze came to Dan's side and sat down. She even looked concerned.

"I really don't know, Grams," he spoke so softly that Helen could hardly hear him. He held the letter out for her to see. "I think you'd better sit down before you read this."

* * *

Helen got a sick feeling down deep inside when she read the letter. She suspected that whatever had haunted her husband for the past twenty years was going to be passed on to Dan. But she was as puzzled as Dan about what that demon might be. Dan was staring at the letter to the Prestons. He reached out and picked it up, turning it over in his hands as though he might unlock the secret inside. He reached for the other letter that was addressed to him and started to tear it open. He changed his mind. He had always trusted his granddad. Now was not the time to stop. He would take the letter to Richard and Barbara, and he would be there when they read it. But he had a feeling he wasn't going to like anything it said.

~ 25 ~

Barbara happened to see Dan standing at the front door. Why wasn't he just coming in like he usually did? She opened the door just as he raised his hand to knock.

"Since when do you knock on our door, Daniel Barclay? How long have you been standing out there?" Barbara took a good look at Dan's face and her smile faded. "Dan what's wrong? Come on in." Just as Barbara ushered Dan into the house, Julie walked up the sidewalk. "Hi, Julie. You come on in too."

When everyone was in the house, Dan just stood by the door. "Uh, is Richard here too? I need to talk to both of you." He glanced at Julie, gave her a quick hi, and looked away. Julie gave Barbara a questioning look. Barbara shook her head and shrugged her shoulders before she walked out of the room to find Richard. It was clear to Julie that something was up.

"Uh, I can leave," Julie offered just as Barbara returned. Barbara was going to tell her that wasn't necessary when

Dan looked at Julie. His face looked more stricken than it had at the funeral.

"I'm sorry, Julie. I really need to see Richard and Barbara alone. It's about Granddad."

Julie looked down at the letter Dan was holding. "Barbara, I'll see you tomorrow morning after I get off work." Barbara only nodded. Apprehension was clouding her features. It was clear that Dan was troubled. Richard came into the room just as Julie was leaving.

"I'm sorry to interrupt. I need to talk with you both, and I'm not really sure how or where to start."

"Let's go into the kitchen and have something cold to drink," Barbara offered.

* * *

The three of them were sitting around the table, each with a glass of tea. Dan still hadn't said anything when Richard broke the silence. "Dan, does this have something to do with the letter you've been pawing since you got here?"

Dan was slow to respond, trying to think of the best way to deliver this message. "Let me explain if I can. A couple of days before Granddad and Grams left for Hawaii, Granddad came home and told us that he was dying." Richard and Barbara gave each other a confused look.

"It wasn't a surprise with his heart?" questioned Barbara.

"It was. But he was very ill anyway. He insisted Grams and I not tell anyone. I couldn't believe it. He looked so healthy at first. And then he announced that he was taking Grams on the trip." Dan took a deep breath. "Before they left he told me that he had a letter for both me and you guys. He said it would explain a few things. He made me promise to give you your letter if something went wrong. He insisted. And then when he got back he looked so bad, and Doc said his heart just gave out on him." Dan stopped for a minute. Richard and Barbara waited patiently.

"I remembered the letters today, after you guys left the house. I've read mine and now I'm delivering yours. But I've got to tell you, mine didn't make much sense. I thought maybe he would finally tell us what made him so ill, but I don't think that's it. I really don't know what this is all about, but it doesn't feel good. He... my letter said that he hoped we could forgive him, but he didn't say what for. I just don't know what to expect." Dan held the envelope toward Richard. "He also asked me to stay with you while you read this."

Richard took the letter. "I don't have a clue as to what it could be; do you Barbara?"

Barbara shook her head slowly. Richard opened the letter and began to read.

> *Dear Richard and Barbara,*
> *If you are reading this, it means I have gone to meet my maker. When you finish this letter you may prefer it that way, although I want you to both know how much I have valued your friendship and love over the years. We have been through a lot together. I never would have made it if you hadn't been there to support Helen and me when Dan's parents died. But now I owe you an explanation of something that's affected all of us over*

the years. I'm a coward—I can't bring myself to tell you in person.

I don't want to bring you a fresh pain. God knows you have had more than your share. This goes back to the night that Amanda, Ruth, and Don were killed. I told everyone that I went to Ruth and Don's house to talk over a problem about Jimmy. But that's not exactly what happened. I went to the house to pick Jimmy up. Yes, Jimmy was there. So was Jenny. Jimmy was hysterical, so I knew I had to get him and Jenny out of there. I took them home to Mom and Pop's place. As soon as we got Jimmy calmed down enough that Pop could handle him, I was going to bring Jenny to your house.

Richard stopped reading for a second as he looked up at both Dan and Barbara. As the meaning of what was being read soaked in, Barbara gasped. She had her hand on her chest as though she had just received an injury to her heart. Richard started shaking so hard he couldn't see the words on the page. Dan was sitting with his elbows on his knees staring at the floor. Barbara let out a sigh, as though she had been holding her breath. She ever so gently reached over and took the letter from Richard. In a quivering voice she started reading, beginning with the sentence Richard had just read.

As soon as we got Jimmy calmed down enough that Pop could handle him, I was going to bring Jenny to your house. I went into the living room to get her.

She had fallen asleep on Mom's couch earlier. But then she was gone. There were muddy tracks on the floor, and it is my belief that whoever the killer was, he came into the house and took Jenny.

On the way back to Don and Ruth's house, I decided not to tell anyone about Jenny or about Jimmy being in the house. I couldn't change what had happened to your family, but I could protect Jimmy. You know how some of the people in this town were afraid of him. Anytime crazy things happened in the neighborhood, Jimmy was the first person who was blamed. I know how much he loved Don and Ruth. He never would have hurt them—I believe that with all my heart and soul.

I have never given up trying to find Jenny. I imagine Dan can tell you that. He has even worked with me. But Dan did not know that Jenny was with me that night either.

I'm so sorry that I'm a coward and can't tell you this while I'm still alive.

I only pray that God can forgive me. If he can't I will spend an eternity in hell. I won't ask for your forgiveness, but I hope you can understand why I did what I did. I'm telling you this so that you know Jenny was alive the last time I saw her. You two have been through so much that I don't want to bring you more grief. I do love you both.

With love and regrets,
Will

No one in the room spoke. They had all spent most of the day mourning the man that they just found out had lied to them for the last twenty-two years. Dan could not look at

Barbara or Richard. He felt like a part of him was guilty for the lie he had just found out about. He couldn't remember much about Jimmy, so he didn't understand.

Richard's chair scraped the floor as he moved away from the table. He stood up and looked down at the letter once more before he turned and walked out of the room. Both Dan and Barbara jumped as they heard the front door slam.

"Should I go after him?" Dan asked.

"Let him be." Barbara knew Richard well enough to know that he needed to handle this news in his own way. She reached out for Dan's hand. They sat in silence holding hands, neither knowing what to say to the other.

~ 26 ~

When Richard left the house he started walking. He thought he might burst if he didn't let off some steam somehow. He had no destination in mind, but he ended up at the cemetery, where earlier in the day he had said his final good-bye to someone he had considered a good friend. Now, his emotions were raging against his so-called friend. He walked over to Will Barclay's freshly dug grave and spit on it. He used every vile curse word that he had ever heard as he ranted. He wanted to reach into the grave, grab Will Barclay and shake him awake so that he could get answers to all the questions churning inside him. Will had been beside him at the worst time of his life. Will had been the one to hold him together when his family was murdered. He and Helen had been there for Barbara when she was falling apart. But now, he'd found out that Will Barclay had been lying to them the whole time.

Richard sank to his knees and looked skyward. "Why?" Richard had asked that question a million times in the last twenty-two years. "I don't understand. Why? God, what have Barbara and I done that you let this shithead be anywhere near us?" Richard's shoulders were shaking—he thought he was going to vomit. He wanted to vomit on top of Will's grave. He tasted bile in his throat, but his lunch stayed put. Tears blurred his vision and burned behind his eyelids. But the tears gave him no relief. He stayed there for a long time, letting all feelings drain from him. He finally got up from his knees and walked heavily to the three other graves nearby. Ruth, Don, and Amanda's graves were beside each other. He knew Barbara came here almost every day to put flowers from her garden on the graves. Today she had come very early because of Will's funeral, and the flowers had wilted in the heat of the afternoon. There were two plots left, one for him and one for Barbara. Oh how he wished he were in his plot right now instead of looking at Amanda's. He knelt on his daughter's grave. He reached out with his large rough hand and tenderly touched Amanda's gravestone.

Suddenly Richard understood what Will's letter meant. Someone wanted that little girl so much that they'd risked following the sheriff to get her! But Jenny very possibly could have survived that horrible day. If she had been kidnapped, it meant that she had not just wandered out of the house that night. He and half the town had searched the swollen creek for fear of finding her body. And Will had known all along that she wasn't in that creek. How could he have let them believe she might have been? How could he have kept that fact from the state authorities when they investigated the case? How in the hell could Will have let the murderer come into his parents' house and take Richard's precious grandchild?

Richard hadn't thought he could ever feel as much pain as he had on that day. But his wound was torn wide open once again. He finally quit weeping. He gathered himself up and left the cemetery, walking like a very old man.

* * *

Barbara wanted to say something to help Dan. Dan wanted to say something to help Barbara. Neither of them knew what to say. Neither of them understood why Will had lied to them all these years. Dan's hero and Barbara's friend had let someone steal a little girl out from under his nose—and then to lie about it! It was incomprehensible.

"That was the demon." Dan spoke so softly that Barbara didn't think she heard him correctly.

"Excuse me?"

"Grams always said that Granddad had a demon haunting him ever since the murders. She thought it was simply because he hadn't been able to find out who the murderer was. But it was because of Jenny. He was responsible for her disappearance."

"I don't know what to say, Dan." Barbara hated to see the reaction Dan was having, but she was incapable of helping him.

"Do you think Richard is okay?"

"I don't know, Dan. I just don't know."

* * *

Barbara finally told Dan to go back to Helen's house. She was not quite sure what Richard's reaction would be when he came home, and she thought it might be better if Dan wasn't there. She thought she should be angry, but she wasn't. She still couldn't grasp that Will hadn't told them about Jenny. Was it because he carried that much guilt around? She couldn't believe that Jimmy had been there that night. If someone took Jenny, then that should have been proof that Jimmy hadn't killed anyone. She hadn't thought of Jimmy in years. He had been a big part of Ruth and Don's life. She would never have thought to blame Jimmy.

When Richard finally came back home, Barbara was still in the kitchen sitting at the table. As he stepped through the door, she was rubbing her temples with both of her hands, as if she could rub the day away. Richard came over and sat down heavily beside her.

"I'm sorry, hon. I would've busted wide open if I'd have stayed in this room one more minute."

"And now?"

"I'm better—not much, but a little."

"Do you have any idea why he had to tell us now, in this way?"

"To ease his own guilty ass! He confessed to make himself feel better," Richard explained. "I'm going to have to see if Dan knows anything more about this."

"I don't think he does. He seemed just as shocked and surprised as we were."

"Did he say something about another letter?"

Barbara nodded. "He said he was going home to read it to see if it made any more sense than ours. Richard, he's hurting pretty bad. We're talking about the man he's worshipped since he was a little tyke."

"I know," Richard said. "And I'm much too pissed off to talk to him right now."

* * *

Helen took one look at Dan and knew that her instincts had been on target. He was holding the third letter as he sat down beside her. He tried to be gentle when he explained what the Preston's letter had contained. She was not surprised at the impact it had on all of them. However she *was* surprised that her husband had lived with the knowledge of Jenny being alive and had never told anyone.

"Are you going to read that last letter?"

"Yeah. Do you want to hear it too?"

"No. But if you don't mind, I think I need to hear it."

Dan nodded, but he didn't read it aloud. He read it to himself and then handed it to his grandmother. His mind was reeling. He didn't look at Grams while she read…

> *Dear Dan,*
> *Now that you know how I've lived a lie all these years,*
> *I want to explain just a little more to you. I know I*
> *betrayed Richard and Barbara, but I don't want you*
> *to think I betrayed you. I'm not trying to make excuses*
> *for letting someone take that little girl, but I have to*
> *tell you that I was in shock that night. Ruth and Don*
> *were my friends too. They had been so good to Jimmy.*
> *They felt like family. Jimmy was in really bad shape. By*

the time I got to the house, I found him standing over Don—I think he was trying to protect him. He had a knife in his hands and was swinging away like crazy. I could hardly get near him. I finally got him to lay the knife down. Then I got him and Jenny out of there. She was all curled up by her mama. I tried to ask Jimmy questions, but he wouldn't tell me anything.

I don't know what would have happened to him if he had been suspected and questioned when the state stepped in. He was never the same after that.

He would just sit and rock back and forth, singing some stupid little tune about Don and Ruth. It destroyed Mom. She and Pop finally gave in and sent him to a home. After Jenny disappeared I went back to the house. It was such a mess. I knew Jimmy's prints were all over that knife and I knew right where he had put it. But when I got there the knife was gone. I always figured that whoever had taken the girl had taken the knife too, because no one ever found a knife. We always thought that a knife was the murder weapon. Dan, I am so sorry to lay this burden at your feet. You know I never gave up trying to find the scum that murdered my friends. If what I have told you helps in any way to solve this case, then that will make writing this letter worth the pain it may cause. I am so sorry to lay this load on your shoulders, but with the tests that are available today, there is always the possibility that something new might be found.

Never forget that I love you, Dan, and I am so very sorry about all of this.

Granddad

After Helen finished reading the letter, she just sat and stared at it for a long time. She finally looked up at her grandson. Blaze had come in and lay down by his feet. The dog's eyes were darting back and forth, from Helen to Dan, like she was waiting for an explanation of all the emotions in the room.

"He would've done that for Jimmy. He always felt he had to watch out for him," Helen said while shaking her head slowly. "He told me how much Jimmy changed after that night. I'd just assumed it was because he'd been so fond of Ruth and Don." Disappointment came through Helen's voice as she continued, "Oh, Will, Richard and Barbara should have been told." Helen looked at Dan and said, "He could have at least told them after Jimmy died."

"I'm going to let Richard and Barbara read my letter too." Dan looked down at Blaze. He reached down to pet the dog and comfort himself. "They deserve to hear all of it."

~ 27 ~

Julie was putting the last of the dishes into the dishwasher at the inn when Rita stuck her head in the back door.

"Hey, girl."

"Hey yourself."

"Do you have a few minutes when you get done in here?"

"Give me ten and I'll be out. You want me to bring the last of the coffee?"

Rita got a big smile on her face that gave Julie her answer. When she finished up she grabbed a couple of mugs and went out back. Julie handed Rita a cup as she sat down beside her in the gazebo.

"What's up?"

"Barbara called me yesterday." Rita always had a way of getting directly to the point. "I think she's hurtin', girl. You think you might have time to stop in and see her?"

"I was planning on it. Something happened yesterday with Dan. Do you know what it's about?"

"Yeah, Barbara told me. But my lips are sealed. Gossip is a nasty thing. She may tell you, she may not, but she just needs to see some sunshine right now." Rita took a sip of coffee. "Now why would my body need a hot cup of coffee on a hot day like this? Here you go, girl. You can take this back in with you." Rita handed Julie the cup. "Barbara said Dan kinda chased you off yesterday, and I know she felt bad about that. That Dan Barclay is one tall drink of water, girl. I think he likes you."

"I think he's going to be a very good friend, Rita." Julie answered.

"Okay, yeah, well I just wanted to make sure you were going to see Barbara today." She stood up to go. "I'd better get this garden watered so I can get to some shade myself. Take care, girlfriend."

* * *

When Julie didn't get an answer at Barbara's front door she went around the side of the house to the backyard. Richard and Barbara were on the back porch talking in low voices.

"Yoo-hoo," Julie was cautious as she approached.

"Hi, Julie," they both chorused.

"Come on over and take my chair," Richard said while getting up. "I have some business to attend to."

"Please sit down, Julie. I am so sorry you were chased out of here yesterday." Barbara sounded tired and her eyes had that cheerless quality Julie had seen in them before.

"Don't worry about it. It looked like you had something serious to discuss. Is Dan okay?"

"I'm really not sure. But let's talk about your morning. Did you have a lot of guests at the inn?" Taking Rita's advice, Julie told Barbara about her morning. She embellished a few things to throw a little humor into the conversation, and pretty soon both women were laughing. Soon Julie was asking Barbara's advice on a new recipe. They didn't have anything scheduled for a special event for a couple of weeks, but Julie loved the challenge of coming up with new things for Willow to try.

"How about we go to the store and we try that for tonight's dinner?" Barbara asked.

"Sounds good. I always like to experiment on Richard." But at the mention of Richard's name Barbara's face clouded again.

"Julie, Richard is taking care of some unpleasant business today. Don't be hurt if he's not his normal self." Barbara tried to shake off the worry. "Now, let's write a list and go to the store."

* * *

Richard walked into the sheriff's office with one nagging question on his mind. He needed to know if it was true that Dan knew nothing of Jenny being kidnapped from Will's house. He had reread the letter from Will so many times his head was spinning.

When Dan saw who was standing in the outer office, he got up to greet Richard by telling Jolene to take a break.

Because she had taken a break not ten minutes before, she started to question him. Then she saw the look on both men's faces. She grabbed her purse and headed for the Creek's Café, nodding a greeting to Richard as she walked past him.

"Come on back to my office, Richard." Dan looked at the familiar envelope Richard was holding. "Have a chair." Richard lowered himself into the chair while Dan sat on the edge of the desk, where he was closer to his friend. "What do you want to know? I'll help you if I can."

"This letter," Richard said as he unfolded it, "it says that you worked with Will to try to find Jenny. Did you know she was alive—well, for a while, anyway?"

"Richard, Grams and I talked this over last night." Dan was rubbing his chin as though there might be a secret he could pull out of it. "Whenever Granddad pulled out that file, which was whenever things were slow, I always saw a shadow come over him. I thought it was guilt that he had let the murders happen in his town, under his watch." Dan stopped for a minute because he was unsure of his own words. "I guess I have to tell you, no. I did not know about her being alive. I didn't even know about Jimmy being there. What I was told was that…I'm sorry, Richard…I was told there was so much blood in that kitchen, and because of the rain, so much mud being tracked into the house, that most of the evidence was compromised. Now that I've read Granddad's letters I think he was one of the reasons the evidence was messed up. As—"

The phone rang just as Dan was going to explain more. Jolene wasn't out front, so he had to answer it. Before he did he reached into his pocket and brought out his last letter from his granddad. He handed it to Richard and then answered the phone. Richard unfolded the letter and read while Dan talked. Dan finished the call and waited patiently while Richard continued reading. When Richard finished he reached up and pinched the bridge of his nose. The two tears that were hanging there finally fell, but no more followed.

"This helps me to understand a little better. I don't like it at all. It stinks to damnation! But I remember how much some people were afraid of Jimmy. I don't think he could have hurt any of them, but I guess we'll never really know, will we? But then who took the knife? Who took my grandbaby?" The two men looked at each other—neither had an answer. "Dan, can I show this to Barbara?"

Dan was about to say yes, when his training stepped in. "I'll make a copy for you, Richard. I'd probably better get a copy of your letter too. These letters should be put in the case file. Since Granddad's gone now, these are the only evidence we have of his actions that night. The state might open up an investigation again since we have new evidence. But it's a long shot."

Richard stood up and extended his hand to Dan. As Dan took it, Richard pulled him close and embraced him, saying in almost a whisper, "One thing I learned a while back about this. I can't carry it all. I have to let go—for Barbara's sake and my sanity. I have to go on with life.

~ 28 ~

It had been several weeks since Will Barclay's funeral. Richard and Barbara had never revealed to Julie what had been so upsetting in Dan's news, but she knew that it had affected all of them deeply. Since Julie didn't want to add any more stress to Barbara's life, she didn't feel like she should confide her own problems to her yet. But she was concerned that by now her parents would be worrying about her. Maybe she wanted Katherine to worry about her. Maybe she was so hurt because her mother hadn't immediately jumped to her defense when she talked to her about Stan. But Katherine should never have called him. Stan had gotten really abusive when he found out she had talked to Katherine about him.

She sat on the edge of her bed and punched her father's cell phone number into the prepaid cell phone she had bought. She got his voicemail. She hung up. Katherine's last words to her still stung. She wouldn't try her. How much courage did it take to leave a message on her father's phone? She punched in her father's number again, but this time she managed enough courage to leave a short message, "Hi,

Dad. It's your daughter. Just wanted to let you know I'm fine. I'll try to call you again, soon. Bye."

Her palms were clammy when she clicked off. She heard a now-familiar noise and looked over at HoHo. He was rocking wildly on top of the dresser. She hopped off the edge of the bed, grabbed the toy, and put him on his side inside her top dresser drawer. *How crazy is that? He's just a little wooden toy.* She was standing there, just staring at him, when the doorbell made her jump.

* * *

Julie was still trying to put HoHo's actions out of her mind when she opened the front door. It was her day off, so she hadn't gone to the inn today. She couldn't imagine who would be here so early. To her delighted surprise, it was Barbara, holding a bouquet of red and pink cosmos. She held them out for Julie.

"Oh, how beautiful!" Julie exclaimed as she took the flowers. "I love cosmos; they're so delicate and whimsical."

"They were one of Amanda's favorites." Barbara smiled.

"Come on in. I was having a lazy morning," Julie lied. She couldn't very well tell Barbara that she was having a morning of anxiety trying to call her own father. Or she couldn't very well tell her that a little toy rocking horse had just flipped her brain around for a while.

"I could use a cold drink," Barbara hinted. "It's hot outside already. Then again, what do I expect? I live in Kansas."

"Oh good, I've got something brewing in the fridge that I was going to try this morning. I can get your opinion too. Willow is having a luncheon next week at the inn, and she wanted something different for a drink."

The two women walked into the kitchen. Julie put the cosmos into a vase, so happy that Barbara had broken the mood of trepidation she had felt earlier. Barbara seemed to be in a lighter frame of mind too.

"Did I ever tell you about this wonderful woman who used to be my mother's housekeeper?" As she asked Barbara that question she knew she hadn't told her about Maude. She had been careful not to tell Barbara anything about her past. She had decided to start telling her little pieces once in awhile.

"No, you've never mentioned a housekeeper to me."

"My mother was not a cook, or much of a housekeeper for that matter. Anyway, Maude, that was her name, was from somewhere in the South. She used to make me this drink that I just loved. She called it lemon milk."

"Okay…" Barbara sounded skeptical.

"It was soooo good. I watched her make it, but I'm not sure I have it down quite right. I need another opinion before I try it out on Willow."

Julie mixed the concoction while they talked about Willow's increasing success at the inn.

"You know, Rita told me that Willow had to turn down a few requests because she was starting to book too many parties. She also said that you are part of the reason."

Julie could feel herself warm at the compliment. "I'm truly having fun working there," she said. She set a beautiful refreshment in front of Barbara.

Barbara took a timid sip and looked up with a grin. "Julie, you have another winner here. Oh, this is wonderful! Maybe just a tad bit too sweet, but it almost tastes like a cross between a lemon sherbet and a soda fountain drink."

As they sat and enjoyed their drink, Julie explained how she'd made it, extremely pleased with herself that she could remember one of her childhood favorites. The subject changed to Barbara's childhood and then to Shady Creek.

"Julie, what on earth made you choose to make your life in Shady Creek? You sound like a refined city girl, and here you are in a tiny little town in the middle of Kansas. I love it here because it's always been my home, but unless I'm wrong, you don't seem to have ever known much about small-town living."

Julie needed to confide in Barbara. But she couldn't do that without bringing the mood down. She changed the subject back to Barbara by asking, "Barbara, tell me, what do you love most about Kansas?"

"Well, first of all it's my home. Richard was in the service when we got married. We moved around a lot. When he got out of the Air Force we lived in Colorado for a few years. Then when Amanda was born we got an opportunity to move to Salina, where Richard had landed a good job. There really weren't many jobs at all in Shady Creek, but there were plenty of empty houses. So we found our house, decided to buy it, and Richard drove back and forth to Salina for two years. Then Don bought the furniture store and offered Richard a job, and life settled down pretty good." Barbara took another sip of the lemon milk and continued. "When Ruth got MS, it wasn't so bad at first. They lived in this house until she finally had to use a wheelchair and couldn't manage the stairs anymore. That's when they decided to move."

"Then they had lived here for some time?" asked Julie.

"Yes, they had just moved out and into their ranch house when they were killed. Richard ended up running the furniture store for a while, but his heart wasn't in it after Don was gone."

"Did they have any children?" asked Julie.

"No, Ruth was never able to have children. That's probably why they doted so much on Amanda—Amanda and later Jenny." Barbara took another sip of her drink, and admitted, "I guess I've just always been a small-town girl."

"What else do you like about Kansas? My goodness, if you left Colorado—it's beautiful there with the mountains and all."

"Julie, it's beautiful in Kansas too. Look at the garden I'm lucky enough to raise. Look at the garden Rita has. I know it gets hotter than blazes in the summer, but it's not as hot as all the concrete in the cities. The cost of living is about as manageable as any place in the country, and we live close enough to Salina or Manhattan that we can find almost anything we want. And now with the Internet access that we have— land sakes, girl, Richard is on that darned computer half the day. He loves it. We can order anything we want, stay in touch with all our friends in an instant. About once a month I get a longing to go to a movie in the city, but I'm always ready to come back home to Shady Creek."

"You and Richard have been wonderful to me. I'm so glad I found you two."

"But why Shady Creek?"

Julie giggled and could feel her cheeks turning red. She could at least tell Barbara why she had picked this little Kansas town. "Well, you're going to think this is absolutely crazy, but I let a button show me the way." Julie jumped up from her chair, "Just a minute, I'll show you." She ran upstairs. She opened her top drawer and took out the rocking horse that had spooked her earlier. She walked into the kitchen holding it behind her back. "I needed to find a place to stay. I hope some day I can explain to you why, but for now I'll show you how I came to pick Shady Creek. First of all I needed a place that was not me. I didn't think a small town would be me, but so far I'm loving it here. Anyway, I got a map of Kansas and put it on the table. I was trying to pick a place. This is kind of a silly thing, but I have a toy that I've had since I was a little girl. I talk to it." Julie looked at Barbara to see if maybe Barbara thought she was a little nuts, but Barbara had a crinkle in her eyes and a smile on her face.

"Okay, I talk to my flowers, so it's okay if you talk to a childhood toy—I think." Both women laughed.

"When I picked up my toy, a button eye fell off and landed on Shady Creek, Kansas. I thought, why not—it's as good a place as any."

"And are you going to show me your guru that shows you the way?" asked Barbara.

"Meet HoHo," said Julie as she brought the rocking horse from behind her back to meet Barbara.

Barbara's jaw dropped, she turned white, and a croak escaped from her lips. Julie dropped HoHo on the floor and tried to grab Barbara to soften her fall as she fainted and fell from her chair.

* * *

Dan was just sitting in his patrol car when Jolene called him on the radio.

"Dan, something's going on over at the old Shepman house where Julie Hendricks lives. Someone called for an ambulance and then called back and said they didn't need it after all."

"I'm on my way."

* * *

Dan saw Richard hurrying toward Julie's house too. They arrived at the house about the same time. But Richard didn't even acknowledge Dan, he just ran into the house. Dan followed closely behind him.

"We're in here," shouted Julie from the kitchen.

When the men came into the kitchen, they saw Barbara lying in Julie's arms on the floor. Both women looked pale. Barbara was clutching the rocking horse near her heart, tears streaming down her cheeks.

"Oh my God! Oh my God! Oh my God!" Richard said three times. He went to Barbara's side, and in spite of his arthritis, he knelt beside her on the floor.

"Julie, what happened?" asked Dan.

"I'm not quite sure. I showed Barbara my rocking horse, and I think she fainted. She keeps saying she's alright, but I'm not so sure."

Richard had his arm around Barbara. He stared at Julie through the tears in his eyes. "Julie, where did you find this rocking horse? We've looked and looked through this house and were never able to find it."

"But it's mine, Richard. That's what I was trying to tell Barbara. I've had it since I was a little girl."

"Richard, she called it HoHo," Barbara managed to squeak out.

"Jenny," was all Richard could say.

~ 29 ~

Julie dropped the spatula again. She mumbled under her breath as Willow breezed into the kitchen.

"Rough night?" Willow asked.

Julie hoped she didn't look as bad as she felt. "I had a little trouble sleeping—I'll be okay." She didn't want Willow asking what the problem was. The inn was full this morning. Normally that would allow Julie to get her mind off her problems. But this morning she wasn't sure she even knew what her problems were; she just knew she had a few new ones tacked on her list.

Willow left the kitchen to greet the guests who were already helping themselves to coffee in the dining room. Julie could hear the conversation turn to the usual questions about the inn. She tried to concentrate on the strata she was taking out of the oven instead of the questions that had been asked yesterday. She was so confused. She had lain awake most of the night, trying to figure out just who she was. At first she wanted to call her father and mother and have them explain to Richard and Barbara that HoHo had always been her toy. The rocking horse had stayed in the middle of the table until Richard had picked it up and handed it to Julie.

"Look on the bottom," he'd said without looking himself. "The horse that Don and Ruth made looked exactly like this one. Don carved an inscription on the bottom of each rocker—one side was J.L.P. The other side was U.D. & A.R." Then it had been Julie who was shocked. She didn't have to look. She knew what letters were on the bottom of the rockers. But she had never known what they meant.

"Do you know what the letters mean?" she had asked.

Richard had nodded and with an almost reverent voice he said, "Jenny Lynn Preston and Uncle Don and Aunt Ruth." Julie had started crying then. Fresh tears came now as she thought about the scene from yesterday.

"Julie?" Willow interrupted her thoughts again as she came into the kitchen, "How about I do the serving this morning?"

Julie just nodded at Willow. Willow was looking at her as though she wasn't quite sure how to handle her. "That might be a really good idea. Thanks, Willow."

* * *

Somehow she finished her duties in the kitchen without any disasters. Willow was still with a couple lingering in the foyer. Julie went outside to the gazebo to wait so that she could talk with Willow. Rita was nowhere around this morning. So she sat by herself trying to sort out her thoughts.

After she'd told everyone who she wasn't yesterday, she had told them her real name.

Dan then asked who her parents were. It was when Julie told them who her father was that she saw alarms going off in Richard Preston. He said that there had been a Kingman family that lived in Shady Creek a long time back. He wasn't exactly sure when they had moved, but he thought it had been before "that night." It seemed like everything they discussed revolved around "that night." It was evident that Dan, Barbara, and Richard all thought that she was Jenny. The idea was so foreign to her that she felt like she was in some kind of nightmare. She had gone into Barbara's dinning room and looked at Amanda and Jenny Preston's picture. She looked so much like Amanda. Suddenly she had wanted to talk to her mother. But Dan had asked her to wait. Wait for what?

Dan asked her questions that made no sense to her. Why had she come to Shady Creek? What was her married name? What was her maiden name? Everything had finally come out in the open. Barbara, Richard, and Dan all heard her story. She told them about Stan, how she had talked to her mother, how she was afraid for her safety. It all sounded like such a jumbled mess. She couldn't get the words out fast enough, and she knew she hadn't made much sense. Just when she thought she was getting strong enough to go back and face her past, she found that she didn't know for sure what her past was.

Sitting in the peaceful gazebo surrounded by the beautiful garden that Rita tended usually made her feel better. But this morning she couldn't slow down the thoughts swirling in her head. Tears were threatening again, and by the time Willow said good-bye to the last guest and walked out to where she was, they were gushing.

"Okay, you want to tell me what happened?"

"Oh, Willow, I'm so sorry. I need to take some time off. I have some things to straighten out in my life."

"Okay," Willow answered cautiously. "How much time do you need?"

"I really don't know. You may not want me to come back when you find out what's going on."

"Believe me, Julie, I want you to come back. I've always thought maybe you were running from something, or someone. Am I close?"

"Kind of."

"Unless you've done something illegal, I want you back."

"I'm really not sure I haven't. You need to know this. I've been using false identification." As the words came out of her mouth, she realized the irony of what she had just said. She had thought Julie Hendricks was a fake. Now people she had grown to love and respect were telling her that Jennifer Kingman Samuels might be a fake too.

She looked away from Willow and saw Dan Barclay, the sheriff coming toward her. What kind of bombshell was headed her way today?

* * *

Julie's stomach was doing a flip. Dan's eyes were hidden behind the dark glasses he had on, but he was walking with a purpose.

"You going to be okay?" Willow asked.

Julie nodded. "Thanks, Willow. I don't know how long this will take to clear up. It's rather complicated."

"Don't worry," Willow said. "Barbara and Mom always help out in a pinch." She got up to leave. "Hi, Dan. I don't know what's going on, but I need Julie as soon as she's able to come back to me." She winked at Dan as she walked past and noticed he hadn't even looked her way. All of his focus was on Julie.

Dan looked at the woman who had been such a comfort to him only a few short weeks ago. He wished that he could give her different news than he had. "Julie, I checked up on Randolph Kingman this morning. I think you need to call your mother as soon as possible."

"What do you mean?" Julie didn't like the sound in his voice.

"Julie, your father was in a hit and run accident several weeks ago." Dan let Julie absorb this information before he added, "Julie, he's in pretty bad shape." Dan watched Julie closely as she turned white.

* * *

Dan handed Julie his cell phone. He was not about to leave her side. He listened closely to Julie's side of the conversation.

"Hello Mother? …Oh my God! …How is he? … Can he talk? …I…I…"

Julie looked lost. Dan was afraid she was going to totally lose it. He held out his hand, gesturing that he could do the talking. She merely placed the phone in his hand, went over to the steps of the gazebo, and sat down. Dan directed his attention to the phone but kept an eye on Julie.

"Mrs. Kingman?"

"Yes," came the cautious reply. "This is Mrs. Kingman. Is Jennifer okay? To whom am I speaking?"

"This is Dan Barclay, Mrs. Kingman. I'm a friend of Jul...Jennifer's. She's had a couple of shocks in the last couple of days. I don't think she can talk right now. May I ask how your husband is doing?"

"My husband is in ICU at the moment. We're still not sure if he is going to make it, Mr. Barclay. What do you mean when you say Jennifer has had a couple of shocks? Is she okay, Mr. Barclay?"

"She will be, but I need to get some information from you. One minute please," Dan said as he covered the mouthpiece. He looked at Julie and asked, "You want to go see your father, right?" Julie nodded. Dan turned back to the phone. "Mrs. Kingman, I'll try to get Ju...uh...Jennifer to you as soon as possible. She's not in any shape to talk herself right now. I need some information so that I can help her get to Chicago."

* * *

Julie's head was pounding. She was consumed by guilt when she thought of her father lying in a hospital bed fighting for his life, while she had been hiding out in Kansas. After she had talked to Katherine, she mentally shut down. Dan was so concerned that he made arrangements for both of them. He was not going to let her be alone. He called Barbara, who helped pack a bag for Julie. With Julie gone, she knew that Willow would need help at the inn, and she welcomed the diversion it would give her. Barbara was closing Julie's case when she asked if she needed anything else. Julie reached for HoHo.

"He's been with me since I was a little girl," she explained to Barbara. "Here," she said as she placed her precious toy into Barbara's hands, "take care of him for me."

"You'll be back to get him." Barbara looked at the woman who she believed to be the little girl she had lost so many years ago. "Julie, I think down deep in my heart that you are my granddaughter, but if you are not—well—you will always be in my heart." She took the horse, Julie grabbed her suitcase, and they both went down the stairs to where Dan was waiting for them. Jolene had pulled strings to get them on a flight out of Kansas City International, but they needed to hurry to make it there on time.

* * *

As Dan and Julie were getting into Dan's car, Larry Augustine happened to be hurrying across the street from Julie's house. When he saw the couple, fear rippled through his body. He ducked behind a tree and watched Julie closely as a memory of a rainy day over twenty years ago came back to him. Larry was sure he had just seen a ghost.

~ 30 ~

Julie looked over at Dan. Neither of them had said anything since they had left Shady Creek, over a half an hour before. Julie could physically feel herself finally relax enough that she thought her brain might start working again.

"Thanks, Dan," Julie spoke softly as she looked at her friend

"You're welcome. Better now?"

"I think so. I really had a meltdown earlier. Yesterday's news confused me enough. Then when I heard the news about my father…I guess I don't have to tell you. When I heard my mother's voice—she sounded desperate." Julie looked away from Dan and watched the Kansas grasses waving in the winds. "She actually sounded like she needed me. I don't ever remember that happening before—her needing me. And the one time it happened, I didn't have anything to give her."

"You're on your way right now."

"But I need to know things from her. How can I…Dan, I don't even know who I am right now. And Stan, what and how do I handle that? I have no idea what else he's capable of."

"Julie, you have a friend sitting right here. I'm going to be with you. Stan will not bully you while I'm around. Okay?"

Julie nodded very slowly, "Dan, maybe you should call me Jennifer when you are around my mother." Dan glanced over at her. For some reason what she had just said sounded funny. He tried not to laugh, but a chuckle came out anyway. Julie looked surprised at his reaction, but she started to laugh too. Nothing she said was funny. Nothing about anything that had happened the last twenty-four hours was funny. But both of them started giggling.

"We don't have time to pull over so that I can continue this," Dan tried to say. He was seriously watching the road just as Julie snorted. It started another round of giggles for her. She was holding her side and tears were forming. Dan sobered quickly, hoping she wasn't having another meltdown. She finally quieted. When he looked at her face, he concluded that the laughter had been the medicine she needed.

"In all seriousness, Julie, I will try to remember to call you Jennifer," Dan said.

"In all seriousness, Dan, you only have to around my mother. I've gotten so used to you calling me Julie, but I guess I won't be Julie while we're back in Chicago."

Julie took a long deep breath and started to relax. She looked over at Dan and asked, "Did Mother say anything about the accident? Did you tell me it was a hit-and-run?"

"Uh huh, Jolene's cousin is on the police force in Chicago. She's getting information from him when she can. I'll keep in contact with her and let you know if we find out more."

"I have so many questions. It was so wrong of me to run away the way I did. I should have called before now. I actually tried to call my father a couple of times the other day. I kept getting his voicemail. I left a message that I was okay. I never even considered that he or my mother might need me. They never have before."

"Julie, do you feel like telling me what it was like growing up as Jennifer Kingman?"

Julie thought for a minute before she said anything. She told Dan that she had always felt lonely. She explained how her father had traveled a lot and her mother had been the one who was always there. But there was always a distance between them. She also told him about Maude. It didn't slip by Dan's notice that she talked more fondly of the housekeeper than she did of her mother. As she went into her teen years and then her college days, she stopped for a second, as though she had just realized something important.

"I had a lot of friends when Stan and I met. And then my friends just started dropping off. I wondered why. As a couple we were always with Stan's friends. I didn't even realize that had happened until after Stan and I were married." Julie's voice had faded.

"You know that's a sign of control, Julie. It's typical that Stan would isolate you from your friends."

"I know that now; I just didn't realize it until after I left and got away for a while. I tried getting in touch with an old girlfriend once, and Stan hit the roof. He wouldn't have had to, because as soon as she found out Stan and I had married, she cut me off short. I have no idea how he did that—made all my friends hate me?" She said it as a question. "Dan, I'm so worried about Daddy, but I'm also worried about Stan. I don't know if I'm strong enough to confront him yet."

"Don't sell yourself short, Julie. I know you've got more than your share of problems right now, but you've got a friend to help you. I'm not easy to get rid of," he said with a smile. "You can do this. Just remember to take it one step at a time."

They were turning north onto I-435. It wouldn't be long until they were at the airport and Julie would be heading back to her life as Jennifer. She closed her eyes and said a prayer of thanks for the friendship Dan was showing her. She also prayed for her father and the strength she knew she would need to confront Stan.

* * *

Katherine Kingman was at the airport waiting for Julie and Dan when they arrived in Chicago. Unfortunately Stanley Samuels had been her transportation to the airport. As soon as Julie saw them, Dan heard her groan. Julie had been so distraught when she had talked to her mother earlier, that she hadn't even mentioned Stan in the discussion. As they got closer, Dan reached down and took Julie's hand and squeezed it.

"Remember, one step at a time. I'm here with you," he said as they got closer. Dan noticed that Stan noticed him.

Stan stepped in front of Katherine to greet his wife. But Dan artfully stepped in front of Julie, held out his hand and introduced himself as a new friend of Jennifer's, looking directly into Stan's eyes. It was a warning. By the time Dan released Stan's hand, Katherine and Julie were hugging each other. Stan was furious. Dan put on an unmistakable grin for his benefit.

"Mother, I'd like you to meet a friend of mine. You talked to Dan on the phone."

"Mr. Barclay," was all Katherine managed to say with a cool tone. Dan was surprised at Katherine Kingman's elegance, even though her eyes were bloodshot and she looked tired. It was clear that she needed her daughter to be with her.

"Jen, welcome home," Stan said taking a step toward Julie.

"Stan," Julie straightened her shoulders, "I'm here because I need to see my father." She looked at Dan for support and saw the sheepish grin that was still plastered on his face. It conveyed the message that she was doing fine. "Shall we go? We both only have carry-on bags." With that she turned toward her mother and started asking questions about her father's condition as they walked out of the terminal toward the parking lot.

* * *

The ride to the hospital was uncomfortable to say the least. Dan had purposely manipulated himself to be in the front seat with Stan. How could Stan argue when Dan pointed out that Katherine needed her daughter's support right now? But Katherine was perplexed with her daughter's cool attitude toward her son-in-law. Dan overheard part of their conversation.

"The day that you called Stan and told him you were on your way home was the day your father had his accident."

Dan turned in his seat to look back at Julie's face. She frowned as her eyes looked into the rearview mirror and caught Stan's look. Dan looked at Stan and saw his grin. It was the look that Dan had seen when he had gone on domestic violence calls. There was no doubt in his mind that Julie would be in danger if she found herself alone with her husband.

"But Mother, I never…"

"Wow! This traffic you have in Chicago is something else!" shouted Dan. He felt like a fool, but it was the only way he could think of to stop Julie at the moment. Julie looked at him like he had lost his mind. And then she realized that maybe she shouldn't say too much. Was Dan trying to give her some kind of signal? She wished she could see his face. She said no more and just listened to Katherine who was explaining how Stan and her father were going together to meet Jennifer when the hit-and-run happened.

Stan was the one who was suddenly talking about the traffic. He pushed his foot down on the accelerator and started weaving in and out of the cars and trucks. No one said anything else for a while. It was a relief for everyone when they finally arrived at the hospital. Stan dropped his passengers off and went to find a parking space. Katherine took her daughter's hand and led the way to her husband's room.

~ 31 ~

Tubes and bandages appeared to be the only things holding Randolph Kingman together. Julie had been holding her father's hand for some time when she felt an ever so slight squeeze. He couldn't speak, but his eyes were open and he was aware that his daughter was there. She stood by his side and looked deep into his eyes. He managed a weak smile. Julie bent over and gave him a tender kiss as she whispered, "Daddy, I love you." A machine that had been beeping with a steady gentle rhythm suddenly changed into an erratic beat. Her father was no longer looking into her eyes, but was looking above her head. Alarmed, she turned to summon a nurse and felt a familiar hand on her shoulder, holding her in place.

"Stan, I want to see my father alone," she said with as much confidence as she could muster.

"Jen, my darling, your father needs his rest. You haven't been so concerned about anyone in your family for the last several months, now have you? I knew you'd come back if your daddy needed you." He still had not let go of her shoulder and was pushing her against her father's bed. As two nurses rushed into the room, Stan quickly released his grip and walked out into the hallway.

"Could you step out of the room for us please?" asked one of the nurses.

Julie surprised herself when she again took her father's hand and announced, "No, I'm not leaving him yet." Her father instantly calmed. At that moment Julie suspected that Stan's sudden appearance was what had riled her father. A chill ran down her spine. Stan had threatened her in the past, but she hadn't even thought that he might go after someone she loved. Why had Stan come into the room, and where was her mother? Her mother had said she would only be gone for a moment.

When the nurses finally left the room, Julie walked to the other side of her father's bed so that she could see if Stan walked into the room again. She hadn't waited long when she saw him standing in the doorway staring at her. Instead of letting her fear take over, she stared back.

"If you take one more step into this room, I will scream bloody murder," she said softly but with ice in her voice. Her tone must have been convincing, because Stan didn't come closer. Instead, he grinned an ugly grin, blew her a kiss, turned, and walked away. Julie heaved a sigh of relief and wiped the imaginary kiss away. She looked down at her father who was sleeping now and vowed that she wouldn't let Stan catch her unaware again.

* * *

Katherine entered the room with a question on her face. As she came around the bed to stand by Julie she whispered, "Jennifer, what happened in here? I saw Stan in the hallway, and he said your father had some kind of attack. He said you need to let him get more rest."

"He's settled down now. Mother, I think...Mother, tell me how this accident happened."

"We're still not sure. Stan said they were walking together in the parking garage at your father's office building. A car came out of nowhere and your father wasn't paying enough attention. They were going to go to the airport together. After you called Stan and told him you were on your way home, your father called me. I wasn't home, so he left a message." Julie was shaking her head, trying to put the pieces together.

Katherine stopped speaking and asked, "What?"

"Mother, I never called Stan."

"But of course you did. Stan told Randolph that you were coming in at O'Hare. He gave Randolph the time. Jennifer, your father has been beside himself with worry over you. I finally told him about your accusations about Stan. Honey, I'm so sorry. Your father became enraged that I hadn't told him sooner. He became suspicious of Stan and questioned him about it. Then the next day Stan got your call, said you had made up over the phone, and were flying home..."

"Mother, stop! I did not call Stan." Julie remembered Dan's strange reaction in the car when this subject had come up, but now she knew she had to make Katherine aware of the fact that Stan couldn't be trusted. Not sure what her father could hear, she said softly. "Mother, I never called Stan. A little while ago when Stan came in the room, Daddy saw him. His monitor went crazy. That's what all the fuss was about. Mother, please don't trust Stan—with anything."

Katherine looked weary and confused. Julie didn't want to put any more worries on her mother's plate right now. She didn't know what had happened, but evidently Stan had played games with her parents when he couldn't mess with her mind anymore. Katherine appeared vulnerable for the first time Julie could ever remember. Julie put her arm around her mother and hugged her. *One step at a time—you have a friend with you.* Dan's words echoed in her mind. She was counting on that friendship. Hopefully Dan was somewhere in the hospital keeping an eye on Stan.

"Jennifer, I'm so glad you're here." Katherine finally spoke.

"Me —" the loud beeping of her father's machine abruptly cut off Julie's voice. She looked over at the monitor and to her horror saw a flat line. Nurses came running in again. This time Julie and her mother both stepped out of the way. They hung on to each other, willing the machines to be wrong. Another nurse came into the room, saw them watching the scene, and gently led them into the hallway. When the hospital staff finally came out of the room, both women knew immediately that Randolph Kingman was gone.

* * *

Dan walked down the hospital corridor just as the doctor finished telling Katherine Kingman that they could do no more for her husband. For the first time in her life, Julie saw her mother collapse. This was the woman who had never shown Julie the emotion she had always longed for. Julie put her arm around her mother as a nurse gently led the two women to the hospital chapel. Dan followed them into the chapel, staying a respectful distance behind, while keeping an eye on Stanley Samuels. His blood ran cold when he saw the look on Stan's face. He was actually smirking. When the nurse turned to leave the room and looked at Stan, the asshole quickly lowered his eyes and acted as though he was a caring son-in-law. He went over to Julie and tried to put his arm around her. Her reaction was amazing and swift. She stuck her elbow into his ribs. By that time Dan was close enough to hear Stan murmur under his breath, "You bitch!" For one brief second he thought Stan was going to strike her. As Dan walked over to the other side of Katherine, Stan walked away from all of them, fading into the background.

~ 32 ~

The promise of sunshine was broken as a cold drizzle hastened the minister's words at the internment of Randolph Kingman. Julie felt numb. The past two days had been filled with sympathy callers, making funeral arrangements, and answering questions from the police. Her father's death was now being considered a hit-and-run homicide. Stan was denying he had ever said that Jen had called him. He said that Katherine or Randolph must have gotten something mixed up. It made Julie and Dan suspect that he might have had something to do with the hit-and-run. But no one else, including the police, was leaning in that direction.

Julie was in a delicate place. She wasn't sure who she really was. She knew she was no longer Jen Samuels. That was Stan's wife, and she was going to rid herself of that title as soon as legally possible. Right now she was living the role of Jennifer Kingman, but she didn't know if that was real either. Could she possibly be Jenny Preston? If she was, what did that make her father? She had truly loved the man who would have given her the answers. He couldn't have been a kidnapper—he certainly couldn't have been a murderer—he was her father. As she said her final good-bye to him, she turned her attention to her mother. They both had questions that needed answers.

* * *

Stan was watching from a distance, building a rage that he knew he had to keep under control. He was being treated as though he was not even part of the family. Jen wouldn't have anything to do with him. What the hell were people going to think when they saw that hayseed get into the family car with Jen and Katherine? Stan had to drive his own car, like he was some kind of leper, not good enough for the precious Kingman family. Jen was still his wife. He would never let it be any other way. He knew he had been right—that if her daddy needed her she would come back. He was a patient man. He had plans for Jen. She'd know how it felt to be an outcast. He smiled at his own cunning as he followed the limousine from the cemetery.

* * *

It was late in the day by the time Julie, Dan, and Katherine got back to the Kingman house. Julie had insisted that Dan stay at the house with her and Katherine. She thought Katherine finally understood her fear of Stan. Katherine told her daughter that she would like to have her live with her while she decided what she was going to do about him.

"Mother, I can't ever go back to Stan. As a matter of fact, I want to go back to Shady Creek with Dan."

"Jennifer, you're still married. Until you're not, I don't think you should go back with Dan."

"Mother," Julie was trying to keep her voice calm, "Dan and I are good friends. We aren't lovers. But I have to talk to you about some things that happened while I was gone. I have to ask you some questions about my childhood and where I was born." Julie watched Katherine's face fade into something she couldn't read. Her mother looked away from her.

"Jennifer, we buried your father today. I can't possibly answer questions like that now." As Julie started to protest, Katherine turned back toward her daughter and took both of her hands in hers. "But tomorrow, we're going to shut out the rest of the world and talk to each other—that is a promise." She looked deep into Julie's eyes, squeezed her hands, let go of them, turned, and walked off toward her bedroom. She shut the door gently behind her, leaving Julie wondering what had just happened. Julie had forgotten that Dan was even in the room.

"I think she wants to tell you something," he said.

"I hope you're right."

Julie was tired and emotionally spent. She told Dan she was going to go take a long relaxing bath and try to think of nothing for a little while.

Watching Julie walk down the hall toward her room, Dan kept thinking how she looked nothing like the woman she called her mother. For the last three days, he had been trying to detect any hint of physical likeness between the two women. He could see none. He knew that DNA tests would be able to prove if Julie was Jenny. But if she were, would she ever be able to piece together her life with the Kingman family now that Randolph Kingman was dead? DNA tests would prove whether or not Kingman was Julie's father too. Dan hadn't lied to Julie. He would be her friend either way. He realized he cared more for her every day.

* * *

Dan still had obligations back in Shady Creek. He went to the guest room and called his office. "Hey Jolene, how are things going? Are you and Ray taking care of everything or do you miss me?"

"While the cat's away—you know how it goes," Jolene laughed. "How's Julie doing?"

"She's hanging in there. After meeting her husband, I can see why she had to run. I think maybe I should stay with her for a couple more days unless there's something urgent going on there."

"Everything's pretty quiet. And you'll be happy to know that Ray caught Jason Brooks with a can of spray paint last night. He was in the back of Tom's store again. I think Ray scared a little common sense into the kid. He admitted to being the vandal. The good news is that Jason's dad and Tom worked out some kind of deal so that Jason could pay off the damages by working at the store. You know, Tom might be able to help the kid."

Dan was chuckling as he said, "Sounds good to me. I'll talk to Jason when I get back too. Anything else?"

"Oh yeah, Crazy Larry was in here the other day. He was ranting and raving about seeing a ghost. He said he knew for sure she was a ghost because he had seen her get kilt a long time ago. I think people are starting to get a little scared of him, Dan."

"Jolene, did he give you a description of this ghost?"

"Down to what she was wearing and doing. It was the day you and Julie took off for Chicago. I didn't want to bother you with it then. I told Ray, and he said he would keep an eye on him for a few days. He said that Larry seems to be keeping to himself even more than usual."

"Jolene, do you remember the description—of the ghost, I mean?"

"Yeah," Jolene hesitated for a minute. "Crazy Larry insisted I write the information down so I could tell the sheriff. Hang on—I've got it here somewhere." Dan could hear Jolene rustling through papers. Her desk was usually a mess, papers scattered everywhere. "Here it is. He said she was real pretty—with kind of red brown hair and wearing a pretty pink shirt with real clean jeans—and she was real pretty except she looked kind of white—looked just like the day she got kilt. But she was wearing a dress the day she got kilt." Jolene kept emphasizing the word. Dan said nothing.

"He couldn't understand why a ghost would have different clothes on, except that she had blood all over her blue dress the day she got kilt."

Dan shuddered as Jolene prattled on about Crazy Larry. He figured Jolene had been a little afraid of him the day he came in to report this ghost. He could understand why people were complaining about him. He had seen Larry occasionally, and he was rather odd.

"Jolene, I'll be home as soon as I can be. The police still have no leads as to who hit Kingman. They're treating it as a typical hit-and-run as far as I can tell. You haven't heard anymore from your cousin?"

"No, if I do I'll call you on your cell."

"Look, about Crazy Larry—if he comes in again, just humor him as much as possible. And let him talk as much as he wants. But make sure you write everything down—to the last detail. I should be back in a couple of days."

* * *

As soon as Dan got off the phone with Jolene, he called Barbara. Her voice sounded strained as she expressed her concern for Julie. "Barbara, I'm sorry. Julie hasn't been able to find out much yet from her mother. But, I have a question for you. This is a long shot, but do you happen to remember what Amanda was wearing the day she was killed?" There was a pause on the other end of the line. Dan knew it was a painful question for Barbara.

"I remember every little detail about that day, Dan. Amanda and Jenny were both wearing blue sundresses that I had made for them," Barbara's voice cracked.

Dan was glad that Barbara couldn't read his face at that moment. "Thanks, Barbara. I'm sorry to have to ask you about that day."

"I'll do anything that might help us find Jenny. Dan do you really think Julie could be Jenny?"

"At this point I just don't know, Barbara. Julie is confused and grieving at the moment, but I know that she wants some answers too. She's planning on asking Katherine Kingman some hard questions tomorrow. Right now she doesn't quite know who she is. Of course, she's Jennifer around her mother, but when her mother's not around she's Julie Hendricks. Barbara, she didn't have much time to tell you about her husband, but I think running away was a wise decision for her. Stanley Samuels is really not a nice guy. I need to stay with her for a while longer to make sure she's safe. I hope she can get some answers for her sake—as well as for your sake. I'll let you know if we find out anything else. Is Richard okay?"

"We're both okay; we've been through worse."

* * *

Dan mulled over the information Jolene had given him about Larry Augustine. Could it be possible that Larry knew something about the killing that happened twenty-two years ago? Dan remembered that his Granddad Will had told him that Larry had been living in Shady Creek at the time of the murders. Larry was spooky sometimes, but his description of Julie the morning he had picked her up at the inn was sure accurate. She had looked pale from her lack of sleep the night before, and Dan remembered she had been wearing a pretty pink shirt with blue jeans.

~ 33 ~

After her long, relaxing bath, Julie went to her room and climbed into bed, pulling the comforter up over herself. Looking around at her familiar surroundings, she felt secure for the first time in a long time. Her room was basically the same as it had been the day she left for college. She thought it strange that her mother had not redecorated it. The shelf that held her favorite books was still there. It was also the shelf that HoHo had always rested on. Unexpectedly a recollection of an unhappy incident flitted across her consciousness. She had been very young—maybe five or six years old. Katherine had taken HoHo away from her and thrown "that dirty little toy" out. She had cried and thrown such a fit that Katherine had Maude dig through the trash and find HoHo again. She had almost forgotten that memory. She had no idea why she thought of it now, except she knew that she missed having the toy with her—even if it had gone a little crazy on her lately. She hoped HoHo was giving Barbara and Richard some consolation and not scaring the living daylights out of them by rocking on its own free will. She snuggled down into the comfort of her bed and was instantly asleep.

* * *

Julie woke up drenched in sweat; she had kicked all her bedding on the floor. The nightmare that had awakened her was vivid. Barbara was standing on a mound of dirt, holding HoHo in her hand. When she saw Julie, she reached out to give her the toy. But just as Julie was about to take the little rocking horse, Katherine appeared from a fog, grabbed the horse, and threw it into a deep pit. Stan came up from behind Katherine and threw her into the pit with the horse. Her father stood beside Stan, looked into the pit, and started laughing. Stan and her father stood side by side, laughing. Their laughter was still echoing in her ears when she became aware that the images were only a bad nightmare.   The dream had seemed so real. Julie remembered having a lot of dreams when she was a little girl. She could never remember any details. She would go to her parents' room and ask to crawl into bed with them. If her father was there, he would bring her back into her own room and sit beside her bed until she fell back to sleep. How she wished she could receive that comfort from him now. She needed to have answers to all the questions she had discovered in Shady Creek. She hoped her mother would have them.

Julie turned on the light and looked at her watch. It was 1:33 a.m. Katherine had said she would talk with her today. But she and Katherine had always had a wall between them. Could it be that Katherine really wasn't her mother?

Questions began swirling in her head again. She could feel another headache creeping into her skull. She had to get some answers, yet she was terrified as to what some of those answers might be. Reaching down, she pulled her comforter back around her. There were no secure feelings left to wrap herself in. She turned out her light and tried to go back to sleep. It was a long time before she heard someone stirring in the house. Relieved that the night was finally over, she got up and showered, trying to erase her earlier dreams.

* * *

Julie was waiting for Katherine in her father's library. Even though the room had Katherine's decorative touch, it had a very masculine flair. It was definitely her father's room. It held a lovely scent that was a mixture of her father's favorite leather chair and his cologne. Julie had always loved that smell. She wondered how long it would linger before it faded away. Katherine's heels clicking down the hallway brought her back into the present.

"Mother, I'm in here," she called.

Katherine came into the room and looked around as though saying good-bye to her own memories. "You always did like to come in here with your father." Julie just smiled.

Julie was sitting in her father's chair. Katherine walked over and pulled up another so that she could be close to her daughter. She was surprised to see a notepad in front of her.

"Jennifer, I have to tell you something before we get into a deep discussion. I have to tell you how very sorry I am that I didn't take you seriously when you tried to tell me about Stan." Katherine took a deep breath. "And then to top it off, I talked to Stan. You don't know how many times I've wanted a chance to go back and do things differently." Katherine was looking to her daughter for forgiveness. "I am truly sorry, Jennifer."

Julie sat for a long time before she spoke, choosing her words carefully. She had felt so betrayed by her mother, but she knew how convincing Stanley Samuels could be. She also knew that she wasn't the person she had been before. She finally spoke. "Mother, Stan fooled a lot of people. I didn't realize how much until after I talked to you that day. He became physically violent after that." She stopped when she saw the shock on Katherine's face.

"That was my fault, wasn't it?"

"I will admit, I was hurt and felt like I had nowhere to go. That's when I started making plans to go to Kansas."

"I wanted to ask you about that," Katherine said, a puzzled look growing on her face. "Why a small town in the middle of Kansas? I suppose I could see you in Kansas City, but it sounds like you're a long way from Kansas City."

"Because I wanted to go someplace where I knew Stan wouldn't suspect I would go." Julie was proud of herself for that. "And choosing Shady Creek is a long story. I'll tell you more in a minute, but first I have a whole lot of questions."

"I'll answer if I can."

"First, I want to know where I was born."

~ 34 ~

Katherine paled when Julie asked her about her birth. She looked down at her hands as she managed to whisper, "Why do you want to know that now?"

"Please tell me about my birth," Julie went on, "and the first couple of years of my childhood. I realized that I don't have any pictures of me when I was a baby. I need to know." Julie had managed to keep her voice firm even though her insides were twirling.

The silence in the room was deafening. Katherine looked ill. But Julie had to know if there was a possibility that she could have had a different mother. Julie waited patiently as Katherine finally lowered her head and began crying softly. And then Julie knew that her very existence as she had known it was a lie. She wanted to run from the room. She knew she needed to hear the truth, but she was petrified by what it might be. The questions had been plaguing her since she had shown HoHo to Barbara Preston. She knew the events had to be much more than a coincidence. Katherine looked up at the girl who had grown into a woman. There would be no more lies. "I don't know." She managed to say.

"What do you mean you don't know?"

"It's a long story, Jennifer. It goes back to my college days." Katherine sighed heavily. It was the kind of sigh that said she was going to confess something. "Your father and I went to the same university. He was different from anyone I had ever known before. My father didn't like him, and I was rebelling. Then one month I didn't get my period. I was pregnant."

Julie wanted to interrupt and ask if the child was her. Instead she waited not knowing what she even hoped for.

"This is painful for me to talk about, Jennifer, but you need to know the truth. When I told your father, he went into a panic. He was in his last year of school. He confessed that he had one child already, and he couldn't have another one right then."

Julie didn't even realize that she was crying right along with Katherine until she tasted the salt from her own tears. She was terrified to have Katherine continue, and terrified that she would not.

"I didn't know what to do. I loved Randy, but knew I could never have an abortion. I was going to go home and tell my parents. I was packing for the trip when I started bleeding. The bleeding wouldn't stop. I ended up in the hospital and lost the baby. Something was very, very wrong. I also lost part of me. When I woke up I was informed that I'd had a complete hysterectomy. I felt so empty. Not only had I lost the child I was carrying, but I could never have another child of my own."

Katherine had a far away look on her face. Julie had not expected this answer.

"What about me?" Julie whispered.

"I'll tell you what I know."

Once again icy fear ran up Julie's spine. Julie needed answers. She had speculated so many scenarios over the past week that her imagination was spent. She could see concern in Katherine's face. She wiped her runny nose and nodded.

"After Randy graduated," Katherine began.

Julie held up her hand. "Wait, I've never heard you call Daddy 'Randy' before."

"Jennifer, your father was a different man back then. He was more of a Randy than a Randolph. When I first met him, he was more like the guy that you knew as your dad. Then his parents divorced and he changed. He became rebellious. He started experimenting with drugs. I was devastated after I lost my baby. We were both like two lost souls. I did some things I would rather not remember too."

"Okay, but again, where do I come in?"

"After your father graduated, he accepted a job from a firm here in Chicago. I really don't know how he landed that job, but it was a pretty good position at the time. I'd come back to Chicago and lived with my parents for a while. I was still messed up. My parents were so disappointed in me. Of course when the hospital had to do the hysterectomy, my parents found out about my pregnancy and blamed Randy. I finally moved out of their house into a little apartment of my own."

"Did Daddy move in with you?"

"As soon as he graduated, before he started his new job. Then he said he had some unfinished business to take care of. He took off. I had no idea where he had gone. I waited for him, sick with worry that I would never see him again. When he finally showed up on my doorstep, you were with him."

Julie was afraid to ask, "When—when was that?"

"It was in the summer," Katherine was counting the years. "It was exactly twenty-two years ago."

Julie started shaking. Her brain was racing. Surely her father had found her abandoned somewhere. A picture of Barbara collapsing when she showed her HoHo kept flashing in her mind.

Julie heard Katherine's distress, as her mother kept repeating her name, "Jennifer. Jennifer. Jennifer, are you okay?"

Julie could only nod and whisper, "Go on. Please tell me everything Katherine."

"Jennifer, you don't look so good. I'm so sorry."

"Katherine, I have to have the answer!" Julie hadn't meant to sound quite so hard.

Katherine went on, "Well when he showed up I was entirely shocked. He told me that you were his daughter, from a previous lifetime. You were two years old and cute as a button. All you had in the world was yourself, some mismatched clothes, and that stupid little rocking horse that you clung to so desperately. He told me that your mother could not care for you anymore so you'd be part of his life now. I assumed that your mother had neglected you since you had a black-and-blue bump on your forehead that looked about a week old. He knew how devastated I had been when I lost my baby. He knew how much I wanted children someday, but that I could never have a child of my own. He said we could be a family."

Katherine was overflowing with tears now. "Jennifer, he made me promise to never tell you this. He said you needed to feel wanted and a part of our lives. Your father was no longer the Randy that I knew. I could tell he was clean and sober. He was changed, and I knew if I didn't accept his conditions, I would lose him."

Julie was somber when she asked, "Why do you think he wouldn't talk about the past at all? Did he ever talk about my birth mother? Do you have any idea where I was born? Did you ever try to find out?"

"It was a taboo subject with your father. I lived in fear that your real mother might show up anytime and want you back. I tried not to worry about that. I'm so sorry, because I think it kept me from being the mother that you needed so desperately. I tried—I really tried Jennifer. I wanted you to have the best. I'll feel forever guilty that when you came to me about Stan I didn't understand and help you. You have never asked about your childhood before. I was always so concerned that you would. I also knew that I would have to send you to your father when you did. And now…"

Neither woman spoke for some time, each caught up in her own thoughts. Julie had the thoughts of a scared little girl who had seen her mother murdered—could she have been that little girl? If so, what else had she seen? She pictured herself as that two-year-old, clinging to a little wooden rocking horse—the only thing that was familiar to her.

"Jennifer?" Julie did not answer immediately.

"Jennifer, are you okay?" Katherine asked with care and anxiety showing on her face. "What happened to you when you disappeared from our lives? Not all of this was a surprise to you, was it?"

Julie only nodded her head at first. She held up her hand now to show Katherine that she needed a minute. How could she tell this woman that the man that she loved as her father and the man that Katherine loved as her husband may have been involved in a murder that happened so long ago? How could she tell her that she may have found out about her birth mother only to lose her to the memory of a tragedy? Looking into Katherine's eyes, she could now understand some of Katherine's complexities. Julie purposefully gave her a gift, addressing her as Mother.

"Mother, I have a story to tell you of where I have been. Please help me fill in some of the pieces if you can. I need to know. I need to know if I was the little girl I've heard so much about the last couple of months."

* * *

The next couple of hours were filled with Julie telling Katherine about her life as Julie Hendricks. Katherine was shocked and dismayed. When Julie related the day Barbara Preston had discovered HoHo, Katherine looked ill again.

She kept repeating, "Oh my God, Jennifer!"

"Is there anything you know about this, Katherine?"

"It explains a question I've always had," she said. "It absolutely never made any sense to me before. Your father used to have horrible nightmares when we were first married. He sometimes would yell out in his sleep, always saying the same thing. "No! No! Let that damned horse stay here!" Then he would say, "Okay, little baby. Its okay, you can have it."

~ 35 ~

It had been a tearful good-bye when Katherine took Dan and Julie to the airport. Katherine had insisted that she would be fine.

"Of course I don't want you to go, but you have to. Besides I know that Mr. Barclay needs to leave, and if he leaves without you I think Stan might try to get to you. Jennifer, I think you need to get away from him. I'll help you in any way I can. I wish you would start the legal procedures right away."

"Thanks, Katherine. Please be careful when it comes to Stan. I need to find out who I am, and then I'll deal with Stan. I have to take this one day at a time."

"I'm proud of you," Katherine had said. "Jennifer, when you were a little girl I always wanted you to call me Mommy and you never would. You wouldn't even call me Mother until you were older. I always had your mother pictured as some despicable person who didn't care about you, but now…" She stopped talking and embraced Julie.

Julie knew how independent Katherine could be, but until her father's death, she had never seen the vulnerable side of her before. It endeared her to the woman she had usually called Katherine. It was ironic that when she found out Katherine wasn't her birth mother, she felt closer to her than she ever had before. Her parting words to Katherine at the airport had been, "Bye, Mommy." No one needed to say anything more.

* * *

Julie and Dan had kept the conversation light as they waited to board their flight. Dan was amazed at the woman who sat next to him. Her world had turned upside-down and topsy-turvy. The truths that were coming out were not always pleasant. But she had told him that she was determined to never be a victim again. When she had filled him in on the details of what Katherine had told her, he suspected that Julie being the real Jenny Preston was a good probability. How he wished his granddad were still alive so that he could get a few more answers. The thought of what his granddad had done stung him. Julie started to ask him a question just as their boarding was announced. They were right under a speaker and he hadn't heard a word she'd said. But she had already gathered herself up to stand in line for boarding.

* * *

Julie had loved to fly since her childhood when her father had taken her to Disneyland. She settled into the window seat and could hardly wait for takeoff. But her thoughts kept returning to the night before. Dan had been asking Katherine for little bits and pieces of Jennifer's childhood. Julie had left the room for a short time and when she had come back, she had overheard part of their conversation.

"I know it was a long time ago, Mrs. Kingman, but do you happen to remember if the…uh if Jennifer had a little blue sundress?"

"She did not."

"You're sure of that?"

"Absolutely! The reason I'm sure is that she had no dresses at all. She had hardly any clothes with her, and they were mostly jeans and T-shirts—you know, more like a little boy's clothes. Her hair was chopped short. She was cute as a button, but she needed…I always thought maybe her mother had neglected her. Randolph wouldn't talk about it. He made it perfectly clear that if I wanted him, I accepted his daughter the way she was and didn't ask questions." As Julie had walked into the room, Katherine had smiled at her and continued, "Mr. Barclay, I had a few sins of my own back then. I loved Jennifer's father, and I knew I could never have a child of my own. I accepted the conditions and the daughter."

As Julie thought about that dialogue, she didn't like the implications about her father. Settled comfortably into her seat, she turned and asked, "Why were you asking Katherine about a sundress, Dan? Was Jenny wearing a sundress the day she disappeared?"

The plane had taxied to the end of the runway and was starting to lift off. Dan answered thoughtfully when they were up in the air. "Yeah, she had on a little blue sundress. It's something I just found out about, and I'm not sure if it means anything or not. Let me look into it, and then I'll tell you about it."

"This has been left unsaid by everyone, but Dan, the implication is there. My father may have been responsible for those murders." There. She had said it. She didn't like it one bit. "I can't believe that about him." She turned away and looked at the clouds that were floating lazily below the airplane. She remembered how excited she had been on that first trip when she saw that sight—how her father and she had both had such a fun trip. Funny, she didn't remember Disneyland that much, but she remembered that flight with her father. She felt Dan's light touch on her arm.

"Julie, I understand what you mean about your father. I adored my granddad. He was my hero for most of my life. Well, except for the part where I was a know-it-all, testosterone-charged teenager." Dan stopped talking until Julie turned and looked into his eyes. Dan continued, "When Granddad died, he left several letters—sort of confession letters. Two were for me, and one was for Richard and Barbara."

"Is that what had Barbara so upset?" Julie asked with a look that said she might have guessed something.

"Yeah, it's pretty nasty, and I'm really embarrassed by it all. I'm not sure how Barbara and Richard would feel about me telling you about this, but well…" Dan was having trouble going on.

"You don't have to tell me if you don't want to."

"Granddad lost some of his hero status the day I read those letters. He...well...he compromised some of the evidence of the murders."

"But why? How? Barbara told me how much he helped her and Richard. She said she wouldn't have been able to get through that time without both of your grandparents' help"

Dan explained the letters to Julie. He told her about his granddad's brother. She could see the hurt written all over his face as he talked. She understood the hurt only too well right now. When he finished telling her about his granddad, he didn't look at Julie for a long time. When he finally did, he found her looking at him as though she understood it perfectly.

Julie finally spoke softly, "You were lied to, too, by someone you loved. And he was trying to protect someone he loved. Maybe I'm just not grown-up enough to understand any of this." Julie sank back into her seat. Neither of them said much more on the short flight back to Kansas City.

~ 36 ~

Both Dan and Julie agreed to steer clear of serious conversation for the rest of the day. They had stopped in Topeka and had a pleasant lunch before they got back on the interstate for the last leg of their trip. Back in the car again, Julie made the remark that she had some misconceptions about Kansas.

"What kind of misconceptions?"

"Well, I thought the land would be flatter, and I suppose I thought I would have to watch out for a tornado every other day."

Dan started laughing. "Watch the movie that made Kansas famous, did you?"

"Maybe." Julie didn't know whether to admit it or not. She decided to focus on the scenery instead. "Were the colors this brilliant when we traveled this road a couple of days ago?"

"Probably not. Our thoughts weren't exactly on the scenery back then."

"I guess not," Julie said, thinking that she didn't want to think about any of that right now. "Dan, do you run every morning?"

"Yeah. Whenever I can. Man it will feel good to get back to that again. I especially like to run this time of the year when the mornings are crisp and the colors are so vibrant. Have you ever tried it? It's a great stress reliever."

"I did when I was a teenager. I went through a little rebellion stage. I coped by running. I worked out a lot of aggression that way. Of course Katherine insisted I run at the gym. She never wanted me to be in any of the parks—it was too dangerous. I did though. I did it quite a few times that she didn't know about. Then I found out she was probably right. Some creep started following me one day. Scared the rebellion right out of me, and I didn't ever try that again."

"Have you ever seen the running and bike path we have in Shady Creek?"

"No. Is that where you go every morning?"

"Yeah. It's pretty nice. It runs parallel to the old highway. That's where Blaze and I head off to after we meet you walking to work."

"Will you show me where it is? I have a pair of running shoes that haven't seen much wear except on my walk to the inn." Julie felt a positive note nudge her consciousness. "I remember how much stronger I felt as a teenager when I ran. I think I could use a dose of that feeling right now."

Dan smiled and looked over at her. Julie was starting to amaze him. She had a lot of turmoil going on in her life, but she wasn't wasting time feeling sorry for herself. "Would you like a running partner?" He had a twinkle in his eye, like the twinkle he always got when he said something to tease her.

"You would run twice a day? Because I can't go when there are hungry people at the inn."

"I wasn't thinking of me. But Blaze would certainly love it."

"Perfect! I would love to have her go with me."

"We'll see what we can work out. Between Grams, Richard, and Barbara taking care of her, she's probably pretty spoiled right now. But she's probably missed the morning jaunts."

"She won't get much out of me until I get into shape, but when I do... Can we start tomorrow?"

"We should have plenty of time for me to show you the running path when we get back today. I know Richard and Barbara are going to have lots of questions for you to answer though. Do you want to talk to them first or take Blaze out to the path?"

"I think we need to talk to Richard and Barbara. I know they're anxious to know everything that we found out. I just don't want to give them information that might be disappointing to them."

"You are a wise woman, Julie Hendricks or Jennifer Kingman or Jenny Preston. Whoever you are, I think Richard and Barbara already love you. You're right though, we can't give them false hope." Dan spoke the words as he flipped his turn signal on and got on the exit ramp for Shady Creek.

* * *

Blaze announced Dan and Julie's arrival as soon as their car turned in the drive. She happened to be staying at Richard and Barbara's house today. She loved Richard and Barbara, but she was ecstatic when she heard Dan's voice. The minute Barbara opened the front door, she bounded across the yard to greet her master. She jumped back and forth between Julie and Dan, showing everyone how pleased she was. Barbara hung back, not wanting to interrupt the dog's enthusiastic welcome. Even though she had been talking to either Dan or Julie every day on the phone, she still had questions. When Blaze finally calmed down, Barbara opened her arms and Julie walked into them. The embrace felt like a warm blanket on a cold winter's day.

"Welcome back."

"It's good to be back. I've missed you, Barbara."

"How is your…how is Katherine?"

"She's doing well, thank you." Julie looked into Barbara's eyes. She had already told Barbara that Katherine was not her birth mother, but she hadn't told anyone how much her feelings had warmed toward Katherine. "She wants to meet you…even if you…even if…in spite of what we find out the next several days and weeks."

"I think I'd like to meet her too." Blaze was getting impatient again and trying to get everyone's attention by jumping up on either Dan or Julie. Barbara then did something that surprised everyone. She let out a piercing whistle. She looked at Blaze. "You! Settle down. Let's go in." With that she turned and walked toward the house. Blaze calmly followed. Dan and Julie looked at each other completely bewildered and calmly followed too. Both were holding back giggles.

* * *

Julie called Willow to let her know she would be at the inn the next morning. She asked about the schedule for any special events and was delighted to find out the next three weekends had small events booked. Willow expressed her relief that Julie would be there to help, and Julie was surprised to realize that getting back to work and a routine felt good. Her life had been a constant roller-coaster the last several weeks. And she knew there might be more ahead, but a little normalcy would feel good for a while.

As soon as Julie got off the phone, Dan came in the house. A panting Blaze followed. They had been playing a hard game of fetch. Barbara had already informed them that they were all having dinner at her house, and Helen would be joining them. As a matter of fact, Richard was out getting a few supplies for dinner, "and he'd better get back pretty soon." Dan took the opportunity to call into the office to check in with Jolene. Julie overheard bits and pieces of the conversation.

"Again? This morning?" Dan was saying. "I'll look into it right now."

As soon as he put the phone down, he apologetically excused himself for a little while. He promised to be back as soon as he could, but he gave no clue as to where he was going. Everyone assumed he was headed for the office. He knew it was a long shot, but he wasn't going to discount anything at this point. The minute he walked out the door Blaze went over by the door and lay down. She was getting used to waiting.

~ 37 ~

Dan saw Larry's backside as he slid down beside a culvert in the abandoned park outside of town. Dan had always suspected that Larry used one of the old restrooms in the park as a refuge in bad weather, so he had started looking for him in that area. The VFW and several church organizations in Shady Creek had tried to help Larry Augustine over the years, but Larry wanted nothing to do with them. Dan's granddad had told him Larry's story as he knew it.

Larry had grown up in Shady Creek. He joined the Army in 1966, and was sent to serve in Vietnam, where he was wounded with a head injury. He received a medical discharge and came back home to Shady Creek, where he lived with his parents for a while. He was not the same person. Rumor had it that he'd taken off for California. During that time his father died. His mother remarried several years later and moved to Florida with her new husband. Larry eventually came back to Shady Creek, but with his parents gone, he didn't bother finding a home. He just lived in various places around town. No one really knew how he kept from freezing to death in the winters. The Chamber of Commerce had offered him a small cottage. All he had to do was keep the building in good repair. But Larry didn't want anything to do with it. He never stayed in any one place very long. Will said he had never caught him breaking any laws and knew that several people in town gave Larry handouts.

Then when the infamous triple murders took place, the townspeople suddenly became afraid of Larry and gave him the nickname Crazy Larry. He had been questioned about the murders, but Larry said nothing. There was nothing linking him to the killings. However, for a long time Crazy Larry was a suspect in everyone's mind. He became even more of a recluse. People rarely saw him after that, and he had only recently been spotted more often around town. Dan figured Larry was past sixty years old by now and was probably slowing down a little. But he had come into the sheriff's office again that morning, asking for Sheriff Will. He wanted to know if anyone else had seen that ghost. Dan was certainly going to try to talk to the man—crazy or not.

"Hey, Larry, I know you're in there," Dan said as he peeked inside the old culvert. "I'm Will Barclay's grandson, Dan. Do you remember me? I'm the sheriff now. I'd like to talk to you for a minute." If Dan hadn't spied Larry's backside he would never have known anyone was even around. He waited patiently for an answer. "Hey, Larry, I want to talk to you about that ghost you told Jolene about."

"She didn't believe me," came a reply on the other side of Dan. Dan nearly jumped out of his skin. How on earth did Larry get behind him? Dan turned slowly to look into a pair of icy blue eyes. They reminded him of pictures he had seen of wolves—the same wild look. They were set deep in the lined face of the old man and almost hidden behind his tangled beard and long hair. His clothes were, surprisingly, not in bad shape. But it had been way too long since Larry had bathed.

"She didn't believe me Dan," he said again. "But I saw that lady get kilt. It was a long time ago. And then I saw her with you, Dan. Dan, she's a ghost. You got to be careful!"

"Will you tell me how she was killed Larry?" Dan asked.

"I don't like to talk about it."

"But how do I know she's a ghost if you don't talk about it?" The sharp blue eyes narrowed and pierced Dan's. Dan had no idea what Larry was looking for, but he must have found it. He started to talk.

"It was a long time ago. I went to that lady's house—the one who used to give me sandwiches sometimes. Some other lady was there in a wheelchair with a man. Then the ghost came and she had a little girl with her."

"How could you see all those people Larry?"

"It was starting to rain, so I got close to the house to keep dry and I looked in the window." Larry stopped talking for a minute. His brow creased even deeper, and he threw his hands over his ears. "They started screaming, and there was blood." Larry was pacing now as he was talking. He had his eyes closed as he continued, "There was a man in there and he had this big knife. And he kilt that lady in the blue dress." Larry was speaking so fast that Dan was having a hard time understanding him. He continued, "And then the little girl came in and another man grabbed the knife.

He was swinging that knife—I thought he was going to kill that little girl. But then Sheriff Will came in and took the knife away. He took the little girl and that crazy nut away in his car. That's when I went in and took the knife." Larry stopped pacing for a minute to get Dan's reaction to what he had just said. In an almost apologetic voice he continued, "I didn't want anybody else to get kilt either. I hid the knife. I hid it real good. And nobody else got kilt. And everything was good until I saw that ghost the other day." Larry's eyes lit up again. "She was with you. Dan, she is a ghost. You got to be careful!" Larry looked at Dan like he thought he was a goner.

"I'll be careful, Larry."

"Is she here again?"

"No, she's not around right now Larry," Dan said cautiously. "Larry, was the crazy man the one who killed the lady?"

"No, he came in and head-butted that guy across the room." Larry gave a guttural laugh, then instantly turned serious once more. "I told you—he took the knife away from him."

"Can you show me where you hid that knife?"

"I don't think I should do that. That knife kilt a lot of people. Sheriff Will asked me about it, but I didn't tell him nothin either. He took that other guy and the little girl away from there. I din't want no more people to get kilt. I don't think I should show anybody. I don't want nobody else to get hurt with that knife."

"Larry, I'm the sheriff now. Did you know that?"

Larry looked warily at Dan and shook his head. "What happened to Sheriff Will?" he asked.

"He retired and then he got sick and died. I've been the sheriff for quite a while. I need to know where that knife is so that I can find out who killed that lady."

"I told you! It's that man that came to the house. He argued with the ghost lady before he kilt her."

"Do you know who he is Larry?"

Larry was shaking his head back and forth with a puzzled look on his face. "I only saw him that one time. But I hid that knife so he couldn't come back and hurt anybody else. I told you that already!" his voice took on an agitated tone.

"You did good, Larry," Dan said. "But I need to find that knife now, and I promise you I won't let anyone else get hurt with it."

Larry's eyes narrowed again. Suddenly his shoulders sagged, and very quietly he whispered, "Okay."

* * *

Dan could hardly keep up with the old man as they walked toward the highway. He felt like he was walking in circles. Larry wanted nothing to do with getting in Dan's car, and Dan was afraid Larry would change his mind about showing him where the knife was if he insisted. But they had been walking for a good thirty minutes already, weaving back and forth through some kind of path. No wonder people rarely saw Larry anymore. He was walking in the brush that only he and the rabbits appeared to know about. Larry finally slowed and started climbing up an embankment

that held an abandoned bridge. A new highway ran parallel
to the old one that was only visible in bits and pieces. This
bridge had been condemned to traffic for the last fifteen
years at least, but it was part of the running path that Dan
had told Julie about. Larry suddenly looked nervous again.
His eyes were darting here and there. He gave Dan one long
look as he reached high up under one of the old trestles.
When his hand came back down, he was holding a very
large, rusted butcher knife. He hadn't said a word until now.
He looked at Dan and said simply, "Here."

"Thank you, Larry. I promise I won't let anyone else
get hurt with this knife." For the first time in a long time
Larry smiled. He sighed deeply and his shoulders dropped,
as though they were relieved of a great burden.

He turned to go but looked at Dan one more time. Like
a wise old sage, he gave Dan a final warning, "You be careful
of that ghost. She won't like that knife much." And then
Dan was standing alone by an old abandoned bridge with
a rusty knife in his hand. Larry had once again disappeared
into the brush. Hopefully the knife Dan was holding would
help that "ghost" find some answers in her life.

~ 38 ~

By the time Dan got back to the Preston house, Grams had arrived. Dinner was in the oven, and everyone was ready to hear all the news from Chicago. They had been waiting to start that conversation until Dan got there, so that everyone in the room would all hear the same thing. Julie felt like she was a librarian at story time when she began talking. She tried to relate everything she had learned that might be a pertinent correlation with Jenny.

"Did I leave anything out?" she asked Dan.

Dan smiled, "I think you covered almost everything. But I want to let Grams and Richard and Barbara know that I told you about Granddad's letters." He looked around the room and saw no disapproval. "There's also something new that just happened a little while ago. It's why I had to leave for a while. It's wild, but it also ties into the letters that Granddad left us."

"You gonna let us in on what that is?" asked an impatient Richard. Richard didn't like secrets, and his trust had been shaken since he had read Will's letters.

"When Julie and I were in Chicago, I was keeping in touch with Jolene every day. Larry Augustine came into the office a couple of times in the last week. It seems like he saw Julie and me together before we left. He's convinced that Julie is a ghost."

"You're talking about Crazy Larry, right?" Richard asked.

"Yeah," Dan nodded. "But this gets a little bizarre, even if we are talking about," Dan made air quotes with his hands, "Crazy Larry." He stopped for a moment and looked around the room. Bringing up the subject of a knife that possibly murdered their daughter was not a pleasant subject, even if it did mean that they might find out more about her death. "I tracked him down and talked to him. He thinks Julie is Amanda's ghost."

"Good Lord Dan, she…" Richard stopped when Dan put up his hands.

"Hear me out, Richard. After talking to Larry, I'm pretty sure he saw the murders happen that night." Dan knew he had everyone's attention now.

"Wait, you said this tied into Will's letters. I don't recall the letters talking about Larry Augustine." Barbara said. "I know people suspected Larry when the murders happened, but Will told us he questioned him and…" Dan held up his hands again.

"I think he 'saw' the murders. He described the scene. He described Granddad talking to Jimmy. And he told me he got the weapon out of the house so no one else would be killed with it. I finally talked him into showing me what he'd done with the weapon, and he led me out to the old abandoned bridge by the highway—you know—the one on the running path. It was underneath the bridge, stuck up under one of the trestles. He reached in and pulled out an old knife. I think it may have been the murder weapon that no one could ever find." Dan looked over to where Barbara and Grams were sitting on the couch and noticed that the two women were holding hands. Both had tears in their eyes.

"Dan," Barbara said softly, "did he know the murderer?"

"No," Dan shook his head. "I also don't think Larry would be a credible witness even if he did know him. But given Granddad's letters, I believe what he told me. And it also reassured me that Granddad was right when he said Jimmy didn't hurt anyone that day."

"Do you think lab tests on the knife could show anything Dan?" asked Richard.

Dan went on to explain that he would send it in for evidence, but that he wasn't sure what finding the knife would prove. He started talking about the DNA tests that were being run on Julie and her father. "I'll send your DNA in too. It should prove or disprove that Julie might be Jenny." He went on, telling them he thought the knife had been exposed too many years, and he didn't hold much hope of getting evidence off of it.

Julie was sitting in a chair off to the side of everyone. As Dan talked, an ever so slight movement caught her eye, and her attention was drawn to the buffet sitting across the room. Barbara had put HoHo on the buffet when she had left for Chicago, and he was still sitting there. The movement was the little horse, rocking gently back and forth. At first she thought it must have been her imagination. No one else in the room seemed to notice. She was afraid to ask anyone else if they saw it too. She didn't even hear the rest of the conversation as she sat spellbound looking at the quirky little toy that seemed to be speaking only to her.

She heard a gentle buzzing sound in the distance. Barbara and Grams were already headed to answer the call of the oven timer announcing that dinner was ready. Ah, routine. She needed routine—she needed ordinary again. She got up quietly and went into the kitchen to help with dinner.

* * *

Julie held HoHo in one hand while she unlocked her front door with the other. Barbara had asked if Julie wanted it back, and Julie had not hesitated in her answer. She couldn't ever remember being without HoHo. Her obsession with the toy could possibly be explained if she had been abducted when she was a child. Barbara had not said anything about the horse rocking on its own, and somehow that didn't surprise Julie either. She was beginning to believe that it was all in her head. Even that likelihood seemed totally acceptable to her. But she preferred to think that Amanda Preston's spirit was communicating with her, and that made her admit to herself that she really wanted to be Jenny, for if she wasn't Jenny, she realized she might never know who she really was.

"Julie! Are you okay?" Dan said as he waited for her to enter the house. He had brought her bag from the car and had insisted he would check out the house before he left.

She must have been deep in thought for some time because Blaze had decided to lie down by her feet.

"I'm angry Dan—I'm angry at my father." The words came out of her mouth before the thought.

"That's understandable. But could we go inside and talk about it?" Dan smiled; Blaze sighed audibly. Julie laughed.

"I really do need to just get a good night's sleep. I'm looking forward to going to work in the morning. I've missed it." She turned and walked into the house. Dan went upstairs to put her bag up as she went to the kitchen with leftovers that Barbara had insisted she take home.

"Everything seems fine upstairs," Dan said as he came down. "We really can talk now."

"Thanks, Dan. Thanks for the trip to Chicago with me. Thanks for helping me sort out who I really am. And thanks most of all for being my friend. You've gone beyond the call of friendship."

"It's truly been my pleasure, fair maiden." Dan took a deep bow.

"I don't even know why I said that about my father. I guess I'm scared of the implications about him if we find out I'm Jenny, but I think it will give me a sense of belonging—I'm tired and I'm going to start rambling. I guess we'll have to see that running trail tomorrow. I need to get to bed and you need to go." She hugged Dan and petted Blaze. "Good night, guys!"

As she watched Dan and Blaze head toward the car, she felt real again. She was looking forward to getting up at the crack of dawn and going to work. She waved at man and dog as they pulled out of the drive and was once again thankful for their friendship.

~ 39 ~

"Welcome back! We missed you!" Willow hugged Julie when she came through the back door of the inn. "Are you sure you're up to coming back already?"

"Yes, I'm sure. Please don't send me away. I need you and the inn much more than you could ever know."

"I'm certainly not going to send you away!"

Willow helped Julie get started in the kitchen on the morning's menu. There were only five guests in the inn, but a very early riser had already shown up for his first cup of coffee. Willow joined the guest, ushering him onto the porch and out to the backyard. Julie peeked through the window and saw Willow picking a fresh bouquet for the table while the guest wandered over to the swing in the gazebo.

As she put a quiche into the oven Julie was surprised once again at how much a simple routine helped her cope with her emotional ups and downs. She and Dan were going to go to the running path later. If Willow could find the time after the guests checked out, she needed to talk to her and give her information on her true identity. She had asked Barbara how much she should tell Willow.

"How much do you want to tell her?" Barbara had asked. "Tell her what you think she should know. I'm sure rumors are going crazy in town already—especially since Dan went with you to Chicago. Rita and Willow are good people and good friends. I really think you can trust them, Julie."

Julie felt she could trust them too, however she didn't like the word *trust* anymore. It was a word both her father and Stan had used often. It seemed strange that she had never trusted Katherine, but now Katherine was the one person from her past who was being honest with her. Just when she was starting to get to know herself for the first time in her life…her thoughts were interrupted by footfalls on the oak stairway. The inn was waking up and guests needed pampering. Just as Julie reached for a tray of fresh fruit for the table, Willow and the early riser came in by the patio porch door. Willow was carrying a fresh bouquet for a centerpiece. The dining room came to life with the morning's activities.

* * *

As soon as the last guest checked out Willow took the opportunity to talk to Julie, who was waiting in the garden with Rita. Rita knew the two needed to talk, but when she started to leave Julie was the one who asked her to stay. They walked back inside to the patio porch and sat down to have a serious discussion. Julie did most of the talking, explaining her reasons for first coming to Shady Creek. She wanted to be certain that Willow wouldn't be in trouble because she had given Julie a job. Julie had a written paper with all her current and correct information on it.

"But please, don't call me Jennifer. If you still want me as your employee, I need to be called Julie."

"Of course I still want you. We'll get the records straightened out." Willow said. Julie was quiet for a moment while Willow looked through the papers she had given her. Willow started to get up.

"Willow, there's more." Julie looked at these two women who had become dear friends. "I don't really know how to begin this part. I may not really be Jennifer Kingman Samuels either. There is a possibility that I may be Richard and Barbara's granddaughter."

"Well land sakes, girl you are full of surprises!" Rita held nothing back. "I know you sure are the spitting image of Amanda. We've already talked about that. But did you know that when you came to Shady Creek? It couldn't have been just some freak accident that you popped here out of the blue." Rita stopped talking when she saw the look Willow was giving her. "Okay, do you want to tell me, or did I go and ruin what you were going to say? Land sakes, girl, does Barbara know that? Well of course she does. That explains why she's been acting so strange for a while."

"Mother," Willow's voice held a soft warning.

"Yes, Barbara knows." Julie started explaining. "We...I... Dan is...we're waiting for DNA test results and hoping we can know for sure. It's all a little complicated, and the reason I'm telling you both is that I don't want you to overhear some of the gossip that has to be going around. You may not believe it was an accident that I ended up in Shady Creek, Rita, but it really was. I was running and scared, and I thought a place like Kansas was the last place my husband would look for me. If my father hadn't died I would have some answers, but my mother—the woman who I thought was my mother—doesn't know the answers."

"Excuse me for asking," Rita looked at Willow and then went on, "but was your father your real father."

"I think so. But we're not sure about that either," Julie hesitated, not knowing how much more to say. But she could see Rita's imagination churning in front of her. "Rita, I honestly have more questions than answers right now, and until the test results get back, I go around in circles trying to outguess the—who, what, when, and where of the situation. If Randolph Kingman really is…uh…was my father and I am Jenny, then the implications are…I just don't know."

"Julie, Mom and I will keep this to ourselves. We suspected Barbara was involved in this somehow, but what you just told us is certainly a surprise." Willow looked at her watch. "Oh my gosh, I'm going to be late for a meeting. You take care. I'll see you tomorrow morning, and we can go over the weekend schedule after breakfast then." As she got up, Julie did too.

"Rita, I'm going to be meeting Dan and Blaze in a few minutes. He's promised to show me a running path. I think I might need to sweat off a little of this stress."

"You go on, girl. Do you mind if I discuss this with Barbara?"

"Rita, I think she might like that. Tell her I said it's okay to tell you why I specifically picked Shady Creek." Julie took off without another word. She knew Rita's curiosity would have her knocking on Barbara's door soon.

~ 40 ~

By the time Julie got home, Dan and Blaze were waiting for her. She was so anxious to get started that she didn't even invite them in. While they were waiting on the front porch, she ran in and changed her clothes. She twisted her hair into a ponytail and walked back out onto the porch.

"It's been a really long time since I've been running," Julie said as she stretched to warm her muscles.

"But I've seen you walking a lot."

"Duh! I don't have any wheels anymore. Actually, I don't mind—about the wheels I mean."

Dan was stretching now too, although he had already warmed up before he and Blaze had come over to Julie's house. "Don't you 'need' to go shopping?" he teased.

"Not any more often than I have to." Julie said with all sincerity. Dan had never known a woman who didn't need to shop—well not any that looked as good as Julie usually looked. As he watched her stretch her lean long legs, he came to the conclusion that she probably didn't need to shop much. She would look good in a gunnysack.

"What?" Julie asked when she realized she was being ogled.

"Just admiring the beautiful view."

"Let's go." Julie said quickly. The compliment was not expected. For some reason it made her a bit uncomfortable, even though she decided she liked it.

"How about we just walk to the path and ease into running once we get there?" Dan suggested.

"Probably a good idea." Having suppressed her emotions for quite some time now, Julie wanted to just take off and run hard like she had when she was a teenager. She had to be sensible. She couldn't afford emotionally or financially to pull a muscle and not be able to go to work. As they walked down the town's quiet streets toward the running path, she told Dan about her conversation with Rita and Willow. She knew she still would have to deal with the fact that she had been living with a false identity. But there would be no more running away. She would deal with her problems one day at a time.

* * *

"This is a nice path." Julie said between breaths. She and Dan were side by side while Blaze led the way. She was disappointed that she was starting to tire so soon. "I think I've probably had enough already though. Please go on and run with Blaze. I'll just wait for you two here."

Dan nodded and kept on moving. Blaze came back to see what was going on with the new running partner, but when she saw that Dan wasn't stopping she bounded ahead of him again. There weren't any other people on the path, so after a few stretches Julie found a grassy spot to sit and wait. She listened to the melodious call of a Meadowlark sitting on a fence post nearby. This place was perfect. Her mind seemed clearer already.

Dan and Blaze disappeared around a bend on the path. Julie leaned back and erased her thoughts until she heard a whistle and a call for Blaze. The dog suddenly came running back in Julie's direction. Dan followed the dog at his slow steady pace. Both dog and man looked as though they were thoroughly enjoying the day. Julie was the one who was now taking pleasure in the view. Dan was turning out to be the best friend she had ever had. She felt herself blush with the idea that Dan might possibly become more than a very good friend.

Julie started to get up off the grass just as Blaze raced straight for her. In one quick motion, Julie and dog went tumbling down the slight slope of grass that she had been sitting on. The dog hovered over Julie, her tongue showing her exhaustion. Dan had slowed to a walk to cool down, so Blaze flopped her body onto the ground beside Julie while she waited for her master. As soon as Dan got near, Julie and Blaze both got up and started walking with him.

"So, you like the path?" Dan asked.

"It looks great. Can't wait until I'm in good enough shape to run the whole thing. How far does it go?"

"It goes all the way over to the other side of the old abandoned bridge. The creek runs dry now, so there's pretty thick undergrowth beneath it. It's where Larry had me completely lost yesterday."

"Is that the bridge where he hid the knife?"

"Yeah, up underneath where all the brush is. I used to go there as a kid, but it's all grown over now. The town only maintains the top of the path. I might warn you that Larry seemed to know his way around that tangled mess. I call Blaze back when she tries to go exploring down there— quite frankly I don't want to have to pick cockleburs out of her fur for three days. Are you sure you want her to run with you?"

"Absolutely! She seems to love it." Julie watched the dog walking happily in front of them. Every time Dan said her name, her ears moved back to catch anything else he might say. But she just kept on walking and wagging her tail now and then. "Do you think I need to worry about Larry at all?"

"Larry thinks you're a ghost. I think he's scared of you. But let me know if you see him, will you? I have a couple more questions for him, but I don't want to spook him."

"Sure. What's he look like?"

"A troll—only taller. Believe me, you'll know him if you see him."

Julie wasn't sure about that, but she was sure that she was looking forward to getting on this trail and running again.

* * *

Julie and Blaze had been running together every day for a week. It was the therapy Julie had been looking for. Her spirit felt so much stronger than it had in a long, long time. A shaken Katherine had called her last night. Stan had called her and insisted she tell him where his wife was staying. When Katherine told him she wouldn't give him any information about her daughter, he called her several choice names and hung up on her. She warned Julie to be extra careful. Julie had immediately felt the old queasy fear start to stir in her stomach, but this morning's run had washed it away. How could she have ever let Stan bully her into submission to the point that she felt she had to abandon her own life? But then, if she hadn't run away, she would never have discovered who she might really be.

* * *

While Julie was gaining strength from her runs every day, she had no idea the anxiety she was causing Larry Augustine. He had been watching the ghost-girl closely for over a week. The first time he saw her on the nature trail, she was with Dan and his dog. But she showed up with the dog by herself after that. He knew Dan was okay, because he saw him and his dog early every morning. Then he would see that ghost-girl with that same dog later in the day. Each day his piercing blue eyes watched. He wouldn't move a muscle when she was near. Each day she got a little closer to his bridge before she turned and went back. He didn't want her coming anywhere near his bridge. But yesterday she had gone all the way across it.

Larry couldn't see the ghost when she was on the bridge. But if he moved at all, he was afraid she might see him. He swallowed hard. The taste of bile rose in his mouth from his fear. What was she doing up there? Was she looking for the knife that kilt her? It's gone ghost-girl! Leave me alone.

"Blaze, come on girl it's time to go." The ghost-girl's head popped over the edge of the bridge. "Good girl. Let's go home." Poof! She was gone. Larry could hear only footfalls going back over the bridge to the other side. Soon he could see her again. She was running back the way she had come, the dog right beside her. Larry finally relaxed. He was going to have to be very careful and keep an eye on the ghost-girl and that dog.

* * *

It was the first time Julie had made it all the way to the bridge. The path seemed to end about a hundred yards on the other side of it. Julie hadn't seen anyone else while she was on her run today, but she felt like someone else was there. Maybe it was the troll who lived under the bridge—not an unlikely thought considering how Dan had described Larry Augustine. What would be so odd about seeing a troll after everything else she'd learned since moving to Shady Creek? After all every time she walked into her house, she was greeted by a delicious aroma that reminded her of gingerbread cookies. And then she never knew when HoHo would start rocking away. Yet, as odd as those things seemed at first when she moved to Shady Creek, they now gave her comfort. She was lost in thought as she rounded the bend in the path. Blaze suddenly took off like a shot. Julie let her run when she saw that she was running toward Dan. He was in uniform and leaning against the side of his patrol car. In spite of the wonderful run she'd just had with

Blaze, butterflies started flitting in her stomach when she saw that he held a large manila envelope in his hand.

"Hi," Dan greeted Julie when she got a little closer. "I finally have some news."

"The DNA?"

Dan nodded. "Both of them. I thought you might like to see them right away." He handed the report over to Julie.

Julie squared her shoulders and drew a deep breath. The first report confirmed that she was indeed the daughter of Randolph Kingman. She bit her lower lip and looked at the second report as the tears started to flow. Dan put his arms around her and held her for a long moment.

~ 41 ~

Barbara started to the back of the house the minute she saw Dan, Julie, and Blaze get out of the patrol car.

"Richard! Richard!" Barbara's voice held an urgency that startled Richard. He was in the backyard trying to get the lawn mower started. But when he heard Barbara call, he headed straight for the house without a second thought.

"What is it?" he said as he walked in wiping his hands on his jeans.

"It's the kids. Something's up." And just that minute they knocked and came into the house. Barbara's heart sank when she saw Julie's tear-streaked face. She went to her and wrapped her in her arms.

"It's okay, sweetheart. Whatever the news is—it will be okay." Barbara looked at Dan, but couldn't read a single line of his face because his eyes were still hidden behind the sunglasses he always seemed to have on.

"You were right." Julie managed to whisper. Julie looked into Barbara's eyes. "I'm your granddaughter."

Barbara felt a joy deep within herself that she had not felt for more than twenty years. Ever since the day Julie had shown her the little toy rocking horse, she had believed it. Now she was absolutely sure. Her tears flowed as she threw her arms in the air and shouted, "Praise the Lord! Thank you, God!"

* * *

When the news started circulating around town that the Preston's granddaughter had been found, there were as many versions of the story as there were people telling it. Of course with the good news that Jenny had been found came the unanswered questions. Who abducted her on the night of the murders? Was it possible that Jenny's own father had murdered her mother and then kidnapped her?

People also didn't know how to address the woman they knew as Julie Hendricks. When Julie sat down with Willow and her mother, Rita's first question was, "Well land sakes, girl, what the heck are we supposed to call you? First you're Julie, then you're Jennifer, and now you are Jenny. Aren't you just a bit confused? I know I sure am."

"Mother!" Willow closed her eyes and shook her head.

"It's okay, Willow," Julie was actually chuckling as she turned to Rita. "Please call me Julie—it's who I've become. And yes, I'm extremely confused, so I don't doubt that everyone else is too."

"See, Willow, Julie appreciates that I don't beat around the bush. I just want to know that you're all right." Rita said with a questioning look in her eyes.

"I'm getting there. I have things to clear up. For one thing I'm still married."

"You're going to divorce that creep, right?"

"Mother!" Willow was shaking her head again.

"Yes, I'm going to need to go back to Chicago and get that business started. Meanwhile my mother, Katherine, is coming to Shady Creek next week to meet Barbara and Richard. I'd like to bring her by the inn, and I'd love to have her meet both of you."

"Are you sure?" Willow said, motioning toward her mother. Rita looked pleased with herself and just smiled.

"Absolutely," Julie said. "She'll love your mother, Willow."

* * *

When Katherine Kingman arrived, Julie was amazed at the way she fit in with the Preston family and became a part of them. The fact that Barbara doted on her and thanked her repeatedly for "loving and taking care of Jenny all those years" made the two instant friends. Katherine's fear that Barbara and Richard might think she had stolen their granddaughter was unfounded. It was only when the conversations turned to Randolph Kingman that the air turned tense. Dan had asked Katherine if she had any pictures of her late husband around the time of Jenny's sudden appearance. She'd brought a copy of their wedding picture with her.

Even though Dan knew it was a long shot, he went looking for Larry Augustine as soon as he had the photo.

He knew there was a chance Larry wouldn't want to talk to him, but he thought it was worth trying. Much to Blaze's disappointment, he didn't take her with him on his run on the morning he went looking for Larry. He had run all the way to the end of the nature path and climbed down the steep embankment beside the bridge. He found the area where Larry had hidden the knife. He sat and waited patiently, listening to the sounds of nature around him. Two mourning doves were gently cooing to each other when he saw the slightest movement out of the corner of his eye.

"Larry, I need to talk to you again," he said in as normal a tone as possible. Nothing. He waited until the doves had called to each other again. "Larry, you really helped me out when you gave me that knife. I need your help again." He waited some more.

"Why?" The voice came from the middle of a thick cluster of prickly bushes.

"I have a picture I want to show you." Dan kept the picture in the envelope. "I want to help the lady you saw me with that day."

"That ghost-girl?"

"Yeah, Larry. She's not really a ghost. She's the little girl who belonged to the lady who was killed. She's all grown up now, and she looks just like her mother." There was no answer for a full two minutes. Dan thought he might have blown it by talking about the ghost-girl again. And then he knew Larry was nearby, because Larry hadn't had that shower yet. He waited some more.

"Is the picture of the dead lady?" Larry was standing directly in front of Dan now.

"No, the picture is of a man. I need to know if he's the man you saw that night the lady got killed."

The eyes that told Dan so much about the man he was talking to widened with fear and anger. "Is that man here?"

"No, Larry, just a picture. Will you look at it for me?" Dan waited again. He could hear a runner going across the bridge overhead. Neither man moved until the runner had passed. Larry held out his hand to take the picture. As he studied the photo, Dan watched the eyes. He saw recognition. Larry was staring at the picture when he abruptly held it out for Dan to take it back.

"Do you know who that is, Larry?"

Larry shook his head. Then he said, "But he's the guy that kilt that lady. Are you sure she's not a ghost, Dan?"

"I'm sure, Larry."

"Is that man in jail? 'Cause he should be in jail. He kilt her, Dan. You need to put him in jail, Dan. He's a bad dude, Dan."

"He's dead now, Larry. You don't have to worry about him anymore. Thank you, Larry, for helping me." Dan held out his hand to shake Larry's. Larry looked down at Dan's outstretched hand. A question crossed his face. Then he looked into Dan's eyes and smiled. He didn't take his hand, but he nodded and said, "Good. That's good, Sheriff Dan— it's good that he's dead." He turned and walked back into the hidey-hole he used as his home.

Dan sat for a while longer before he got up and climbed back up the steep embankment to the nature path. He had just solved a twenty-two-year-old mystery, but he had no idea how it would affect Julie. He didn't think he would ever be able to prove that Julie's father had killed her mother, but he was convinced it was true. And he knew that it was the unanswered question for many people he loved dearly.

~ 42 ~

Dan had showered, eaten dinner, and fed Blaze. Suddenly he wanted to tackle the painting job he'd been putting off for months. But he knew it was time to talk to Julie. He hated what he had to tell her. The pit in his stomach grew deeper as he procrastinated.

"Come on girl, let's go see Julie." It was time to get the job done.

* * *

Katherine was the one who answered the door. As Dan introduced Blaze and Katherine to each other, Julie came around the corner from the kitchen.

"Hi, this is a pleasant surprise."

"I'd like to talk to both of you if you have a few minutes?"

As they settled into chairs in the living room, Dan noticed some of the changes Julie had made to the house. It was always a pleasant house, but Julie's touches were making it into an inviting, warm home. He wanted to compliment

Julie on what she had done to the place. He wanted to talk about anything but the subject he was going to bring up. Julie and Katherine were waiting for him to start the conversation.

"I don't really know how to say this," he said. He cleared his throat. "Katherine, I took the photo you gave me of Julie's father and …I, uh…"

"I still can't quite get used to everyone calling Jennifer 'Julie,'" Katherine said nervously. And then quite quickly her demeanor changed. "It's not good news, is it?"

Dan shook his head. He told them both about his conversation with Larry Augustine earlier that day. Neither woman said a word as he ended with, "I think he's telling me the truth. He has no reason not to." Julie and Katherine were sitting beside each other on the couch. They were holding hands to give each other the strength to absorb what they had just heard. "I'm really so sorry to have to tell you this about someone you loved." Dan remembered how he'd felt when he'd read his granddad's letters. This had to be much worse. For the second time that day, Dan waited patiently, saying no more.

"Will the case be re-opened? What will this mean exactly?" Katherine finally asked.

"I'm not sure. So much evidence was destroyed, and it was so long ago. I doubt that we could ever get Larry to testify in a court. I don't know if anyone would believe him anyway. But it all fits together." Dan took a long breath. "I need to tell Richard and Barbara what I found out too."

"Oh," Julie made a small moaning sound. "I mean, I know we all suspected…but none of us will ever know 100 percent, will we? Or why? Why would he have done that?" Julie turned toward Katherine and held both her hands. "I want to go with Dan to Richard and Barbara's house. Do you want to come too?"

"No, I think I need to have a little alone time. They may not feel very warm toward me when they hear this. After all he was my husband."

"And my father," Julie whispered.

* * *

"Who would've ever thought that Crazy Larry had the answers to most of our questions, stored away under that mop of hair?" Richard was the only one who had spoken since Dan had told them the story. "You think he really remembered, Dan, or do you think he just told you so you'd leave him alone?"

"I'm pretty sure he recognized the man in the picture." Dan said. "I'm not sure if he believed that Julie isn't really a ghost, but he seemed to settle into that idea too."

"From the pieces of what Katherine has told me about Daddy, something changed in him after he brought me home. She said she didn't think he ever did drugs after that either."

"You were a powerful convincing little girl when you were two. You had me wrapped around your little finger. Maybe you were able to get through to your father too." Richard put his arm around Julie and held her for a minute. Barbara was unusually quiet.

"Are you going to be okay, Julie?" she finally asked.

"Yes, I am. I don't like what I heard, but I had suspected it. Now I know. I'm glad Katherine is here for a couple of days. I'm concerned about her." Julie got up to leave. "Are we still on for tomorrow?"

"Of course." Barbara answered.

* * *

Katherine was awake and dressed when Julie got back from the inn the next morning. "Who would've ever thought I'd be the one sleeping in until you got off work?" she said as Julie walked through the door.

"It is kind of amazing," said Julie. "Are you sure you don't mind that I go running?" Katherine only nodded. "Okay then, we'll walk over to Barbara's house, and you two can spend the morning together while I'm gone. I'm so glad you like her, Mother."

"I do. And I like Richard too," Katherine said as the two started out of the house.

"I'll come home and shower and see you at lunch. Then we'll go to the inn this afternoon, and I'll show you where I work."

"Sounds like a plan to me." Katherine hesitated and then asked, "Jennifer, are you sure I can't help you buy a car? How do you manage without a car?"

"I'm sure. I manage okay. I have to admit I have a lot of friends I rely on. But mostly I don't go anyplace outside of Shady Creek. I guess now that I'm not in hiding from Stan anymore I might need to think about getting a car. But for this week we can use your rental." As the two women walked to Barbara's house, they talked about the next steps Julie would take to get Stan completely out of her life.

"Jennifer, he scares me," Katherine said.

"Me too, Mother. But for the rest of this week, I'm going to show you my new life without him. It's a quiet life here. Things move slow and easy. I love working at the inn, especially when we have special events. I can't wait for you to meet Willow and Rita." She stopped as Barbara came out the front door. Then Julie and Blaze headed out together while Katherine and Barbara got to know each other better.

* * *

Julie and Blaze ran all the way to the bridge. But instead of calling Blaze to turn and head back, Julie stopped and caught her breath. She stood near the edge of the railing on the bridge and looked at the undergrowth of weeds and grasses. Blaze was eager to get into that patch of nature that housed all kinds of interesting sounds and smells, but she obeyed Julie's command to stay. Julie spied movement as a sparrow flew out of the middle of a clump of bushes. Dan had told her that Larry was afraid of her. She knew fear, and she didn't want anyone to be afraid of her. She leaned ever so slightly over the railing.

"Thank you, Larry, I hope you can hear me. Thank you for helping me." She felt her voice quivering just a bit. "Thank you for giving me the truth." She listened for a moment longer. She hoped he heard her. She turned to

Blaze, "Time to go home, girl." Blaze took off back toward Julie's house.

* * *

Larry had been watching for the ghost-girl. Today was no exception. When she stopped above him on the bridge, he waited. When he heard her say his name, he nearly bolted. But then he heard that she was thanking him. Dan had thanked him too. No one had ever thanked him for anything before. Maybe Dan was right; maybe she wasn't a ghost. He waited to see what she would do next, but she didn't do anything. She just turned and started to run with that dog again. Soon she was gone. Larry smiled in spite of everything. She had thanked him.

~ 43 ~

A manicured gentle hand traced over the name Amanda Kay Preston. The last couple of weeks had been an awakening for Katherine, and the cemetery felt like a necessary part of her visit to her daughter's past. She needed to see where the mother of the child she had raised was buried.

While Barbara and Julie stood aside, Katherine's eyes were full of tears. Julie heard her murmur softly, "Thank you for giving me the gift of a daughter all these years." She turned toward the other two. "I know it wasn't a gift, it was taken from her, but I always thought you were a gift, Jennifer."

Barbara was the one who hugged Katherine then. "There are a lot of thanks to go around, after a lot of heartache. It's time for me to just celebrate the joy of finding my granddaughter. Knowing that she had a loving, caring mother figure all these years helps."

Katherine and Barbara talked to each other as though they had been long-lost friends. Julie reflected on the past several days. Katherine's visit had been a wonderful boost to Julie's self-esteem and fortitude. Katherine would be leaving Shady Creek tomorrow to go back to Chicago. Julie wished she could stay longer.

Instead of resenting Katherine, Julie's new family and friends had embraced her. Barbara had exhausted Katherine's memory for bits and pieces of their granddaughter's growing years. And the night before, Rita and Willow had welcomed her into their lives too. Since the inn had only one guest booked for the night, they opened it for a very private party. Willow and Rita had included Richard and Barbara Preston, Julie and Katherine, and Dan and Helen Barclay. As usual with a special event, the women had prepared the dinner together in the inn's kitchen. But this time those women were able to sit and enjoy the rewards rather than simply serve them.

When Katherine expressed surprise at Jennifer's culinary skills and called her an accomplished chef, Rita sat her straight. "Glorified cook is more like it!" Willow only rolled her eyes at her mother as she took another sip of wine. It had been a very nice night and Katherine had been pleased to see her Jennifer so happy.

* * *

Back at Julie's house, as they stepped inside, Katherine asked, "Jennifer, why does it always smell like fresh baked goods when I walk into your house?"

Julie shrugged her shoulders. "Happens all the time. I think this house talks to me. I'll tell you this because you raised me—I haven't told anyone else—in this house, HoHo rocks." Julie waited for a reaction.

"So? I knew that. I watched you play with that dirty little guy when you were small. You rocked him and rocked him and rocked him. You were always humming some lullaby tune that I wasn't familiar with. I wonder now if it was something Amanda sang to you."

"It's a good feeling to be able to talk with you about Amanda. But back to my confession."

"What confession?"

"In this house I smell ginger cookies all the time, as if they've just came out of the oven. Remember how I used to beg Maude to bake ginger cookies? Barbara told me that Jenny loved gingerbread cookies, along with her Aunt Ruth, the one who was murdered." Katherine raised an eyebrow. Julie continued, "Well, this used to be Aunt Ruth's house."

"Okay," Katherine said slowly. "What's your confession?"

"HoHo rocks on his own here. Sometimes he just… rocks."

"Okay, that's enough. I won't be able to sleep tonight if you keep telling me things like that."

"Oh, but I find it soothing somehow. He hasn't rocked for a long time though."

"That's good—isn't it?"

"Yes, that's good." Julie laughed. Then stifling a yawn, she said, "I'm sorry, Katherine, I've got to get up early in the morning, so I've got to get some sleep tonight. I'm so glad you came here to meet everyone and to see where I'm living now. I'm going to miss you when you leave tomorrow. Will you please come back again soon?"

"You can count on it. I've had a really good time, Jennifer." Julie tried to hide another yawn. Katherine added, "But you're correct, we both need some sleep."

* * *

Julie hugged Blaze as Katherine's car backed out of the drive. She was grateful the dog was eager to go on their run. It made saying her farewell to Katherine easier. She had gotten up earlier than normal and gone to the inn. When she got back, Dan had already dropped Blaze off, and Katherine had packed her car and was ready to go. She had worried about how her father's death would affect Katherine. Then she worried how the suspicion of him murdering three people would affect her. But she had seen a strength in Katherine that she had not known was there. She decided that Katherine would cope just fine. It was as though knowing the truth had set her free somehow. Never mind that—she had a date with a dog right now.

"Ready to go, girl?" As they headed down the street enjoying the rest of their morning, Julie had no way of knowing that inside her house HoHo was rocking furiously.

~ 44 ~

The days were getting shorter and the nights cooler, leaving the air crisp and sharp. Blaze ran a short distance ahead of Julie on the path, leading the way on their now familiar run. Julie's head felt clear. She had learned a lot about herself and her family's history the past week by listening in on Barbara and Katherine's conversations. But as the puzzle of her life started coming together, she no longer felt like she was hanging in limbo. It was time to clean up the mess of her life with Stan next. He was the one lingering problem that still muddled her brain.

It was a little later in the day than when Julie usually ran and there were no other runners in sight on the path. Blaze had reached the bridge already when Julie realized the dog was heading for a clump of bushes at the other end of the bridge. Uh-oh, cockleburs!

"Blaze!" Julie gave a shout and a whistle as she slowed to a walk. Blaze ignored her call and began barking at the bush.

"Blaze, come here, girl," Julie started toward the dog. It was unusual for Blaze not to immediately obey Julie when

she called her. As Julie got closer to the dog, Blaze stopped
barking. Julie could hear her give a deep growl from within
her chest. Out of the blue, a huge board swung out from
the middle of the bush. Blaze yelped as the board hit her
along her side and her head. Her body rolled helplessly in
the dirt and lay limp at the end of the nature path. Julie
screamed and raced toward the still animal. A man in a ski
mask jumped from behind the bush and swung the board
at his next target. The board caught Julie in her midsection
and completely knocked the wind out of her. She dropped
to her knees gasping for air, unable to look up at the man
that towered above her.

* * *

Larry Augustine had watched Julie every day since she
and Blaze had started running on the nature path. He
had decided that Dan was right and she wasn't really a
ghost, because he noted other runners could see her too.
He sometimes heard her exchange a winded "hi" with
another runner. And he watched how she and the dog
interacted with one another. Larry understood animals.
He trusted their instincts, and it was apparent that the
dog liked the girl. When he heard her call the dog, he was
on the other side of the bridge embankment. But when
he heard the dog growl, he hurried forward to see what it
had found. Just as he spied the dog, he saw the board and
heard the dog yelp. Who would do that? Larry hated to
see an animal get hurt. He climbed the embankment to
get a better look.

Larry saw the board swing a second time and hit the girl. He stopped and looked around. Something bad was happening. Larry would not walk into a trap. But the man wasn't looking at Larry. The man had taken off his ski mask. He was saying vile things to the girl on the ground. He reached down and picked up the board again. He raised it over his head, above the girl.

Larry dropped his shoulders and squinted his eyes as he stared into the bright sunlight. Somewhere from deep inside him he let a sound escape that sounded more like a beast than a man. It was a howling sound heard by all within a mile's radius. When the howling stopped, Larry saw red, the color of blood—blood from a war he hadn't wanted to fight, blood from a killing spree he had witnessed many years ago. He had done nothing to help that girl back then, and he had been haunted by his cowardice for all these years. Larry ran toward the man who was going to hurt this girl—the man who had hurt the dog.

When Stanley Samuels heard the wild howl, his surprise turned him toward the sound. He saw something headed directly for him. He wasn't quite sure what that something was. It looked like a man, at least the bottom half looked like a man. But the top half was a tangled mess of gray beard and flying hair. He looked into the bluest eyes he had ever seen. They looked wild and determined. They were looking into his soul. Stan turned and ran.

His fear reached its apex when he felt a sharp pain in the middle of his back. He went sprawling into the grass and dirt as Larry's head butt caught him in his lower back. He tried to pick himself up, to move away from whatever was attacking him. His legs wouldn't cooperate, and his back felt like it was broken in half. He then felt himself being lifted into the air. He felt a jolt. He was floating in the air.

* * *

Larry looked over the railing of the bridge at the twisted body lying on top of the tangled bushes. It was very still. He looked back at the girl. She was still on the ground on her knees, still gasping for air. Larry wanted to go to her and help, but another man was heading toward her. A woman was standing a short distance away beside the dog. The man and woman were looking at him in that odd way that people always looked at him. But the ghost-girl was looking directly into Larry's eyes. It looked like she was trying to say something. He thought maybe she was saying thank you again. Larry's face revealed no emotion as he turned away from her and headed for his own sanctuary.

The stranger who had come to Julie's side was saying something to the woman who was beside Blaze. Julie still didn't have all the air she needed in her lungs. She started crawling through the grass and dirt toward Blaze.

"Miss, the dog's hurt. I don't think you should get too close." Julie heard the man speaking as though he was far away. "Can I help you, miss?"

"Please, go get help," Julie managed to murmur.

"I can't leave you, miss, I'm afraid that bum may come back."

"Please go get help. The bum is no problem. He helped us." Julie saw the man looking around with fear in his eyes.

Julie finally reached Blaze. The woman was now standing over the dog. Julie looked at her and pleaded, "Please go for help." The woman nodded.

"Oh, Blaze," Julie whispered. Blaze tried to raise her head but had to lay it back on the ground. She was clearly in trouble. Julie reached over with one of her hands to stroke the dog. Blaze began licking the air but did not try to move her head again. Julie moved her hand under the dog's mouth so that Blaze could lick her.

"I'll get help and be back as soon as possible," said the woman.

"Oh, we might need an ambulance too." Julie said as an afterthought. Julie had seen Larry toss Stan over the bridge's side as easily as if he had been a rag doll. Julie really didn't care a whole lot about Stan's welfare at the moment. She was more concerned about Blaze. She said a prayer for the dog, and placing her face close to Blaze, she softly hummed a forgotten lullaby. Blaze closed her eyes and let Julie gently stroke her head.

~ 45 ~

Larry Augustine could hear the couple who were with the dog and the girl. He knew they were afraid of him; he had seen it in their eyes. When he slid down the embankment close to where Stanley Samuels was, he knew the man was dead. He was not sorry.

Sirens were getting closer. Larry knew that soon there would be a lot of people around. If Larry stayed, he knew there would be many questions. He didn't want to answer questions. One of the sirens stopped, but more were coming. Larry heard Sheriff Dan's voice. But Larry no longer knew what any of the voices were saying. He had already gathered his meager possessions and was weaving his way through the maze of tangled bushes that had been his home for some time. He never looked back. He just kept walking.

* * *

Julie had just finished getting X rays at the hospital when she finally got to talk to Dan again. By then she was frantic with worry.

"How is Blaze?" was the first question she asked him.

"She's still at the vet's," Dan answered. "She's not responding well, so we'll have to wait and see. How are you doing?"

"I'm okay. They say I don't have any broken bones, but I'm going to be a little bruised for a while. Dan, I need to see Blaze."

"Julie we need to talk about Stan first."

"Oh yeah, did you find him? Is he locked up? Oh, Dan Larry handled Stan like he was a rag doll. Stan was going to hit me with that two-by-four again. He had it over my head when Larry went after him. If Larry hadn't been there to stop him, Dan, I think he would have killed me. Please tell me you found him."

"We found him Julie. He didn't survive the fall off the bridge. The runners that found you thought that Larry was your attacker."

"Oh, no! Larry stopped Stan. Oh my God, is Larry okay?" Julie knew she should have some feeling for Stan, but right now she only felt relief that she didn't have to fear him any longer. He could no longer hurt anyone.

"We haven't been able to find Larry yet. Look, don't worry about him right now. I called Katherine's cell phone. She was on the turnpike already, but she's coming back. I finally reached Richard and Barbara too. They were going to come here, but I told them you would probably be able to go home."

"I know the doctor said I could go home now, but I want to go see Blaze." Julie looked at Dan and knew he was going to say no. "Please, Dan, I have to see her. She was trying to protect me. If it weren't for Blaze and Larry, I can't…I can't imagine what would have happened to me."

"Julie," Dan spoke gently. "We still don't know if she's going to make it." He looked at Julie's face, "Okay, I'll take you by the vet's office first, but then you're going home. You've got a lot of people wanting to see you."

"I need to see her first. Then I'll go home willingly."

"If you feel up to it, I need to get an official statement from you. But we can wait until you're at home. It doesn't look like Stan's going anywhere."

"I guess I should feel bad about Stan." Julie's shoulders shook as the sobs started. Dan put his arms around her and assured her that she didn't have to feel bad about Stan. "I guess I feel bad because I don't feel anything for him," she managed to say. "Now, please take me to see Blaze."

* * *

Blaze appeared to be unconscious when Julie saw her at the animal clinic. But when Julie went to her side and stroked her coat she saw a slight movement of her tail. Julie stayed by her side until Dan insisted that she go home and rest.

"So long, Blaze," Julie whispered to the animal as she gave her one last pat. She looked at Dan as he slowly nodded.

* * *

Dan called Richard and Barbara as soon as he and Julie left the clinic. They were waiting at Julie's house when Dan and Julie arrived. The minute Barbara saw Julie, she wrapped her in an embrace.

"Oh my God, we almost lost you again," she said through her tears. She led Julie to the couch and sat close with one arm still wrapped around her granddaughter. She and Richard listened intently as Julie answered the questions Dan asked. When Julie told them how Larry Augustine had appeared out of nowhere to help her and Blaze, Barbara clapped her hands together.

"Looks like we owe Larry Augustine a great deal of thanks," Richard spoke softly.

"I need to see if I can find him and talk to him too." Dan got up to leave. He knew Julie was in good hands now that Richard and Barbara were taking care of her.

"Dan, will you check on Blaze again too?" asked Julie.

If there had been any doubt before, Dan knew now he loved this woman. "Of course," he said as he left the room.

* * *

By the time Katherine got back to Julie's house, Barbara had already tucked Julie in bed. The pain from the attack was starting to settle over her body, so she took the sedative the doctor had prescribed and was napping peacefully. Barbara filled Katherine in on everything that had happened. Then she and Richard took their leave. Katherine assured them she would call if there was a change in Julie's condition.

Katherine closed the front door behind Richard and Barbara and tiptoed up the stairs to Julie's room. She looked at the woman she had raised as her own child. She would always love her Jennifer. She reached over and gently brushed the hair from her face. Her daughter, Amanda's daughter, had come to Shady Creek to escape her fears. She had found new fears to face instead. She'd faced them gallantly, and in so doing had also found her roots, tangled as they might be.

"Sleep tight, Jennifer," she gently placed a kiss on Julie's forehead.

Hearing an unfamiliar soft rapping sound, Katherine looked at her daughter's dresser. HoHo was rocking gently to and fro.

~ 46 ~

The first time Barbara Preston heard Julie humming a lullaby to Blaze she burst into tears. Julie was so surprised and alarmed that she left Blaze's side to put her arm around Barbara. She had misunderstood Barbara's reaction.

"I'm sorry, I know she can't hear me, but that tune just keeps popping into my head," she had said. "I still have to talk to her Barbara. It makes me feel better somehow."

"Where did you hear that song?" Barbara asked softly.

"I don't know," Julie had answered. "Katherine used to ask me the same thing and I…" Julie had stopped and looked at Barbara, an unspoken question on her face.

Barbara had nodded slowly, and soon a smile had replaced her tears. "It was something Amanda used to hum to you whenever you became upset. It was just a silly little tune that she made up especially for you."

Julie still smiled whenever she caught herself humming the song. The lullaby came automatically when she wanted to console Blaze, even though the dog couldn't hear it. Blaze had been deaf ever since the day Stanley Samuels hit her with a two-by-four.

Julie's physical bruises healed quickly after that day. Her spirit took longer. The first couple of months, she ran the gamut of emotions daily. Every time she saw what Stan had done to Blaze, anger topped them all.

At first Blaze didn't adjust well. She seemed frightened by any movement that caught her eye. When Dan first took her home, Julie was with him. But the minute Julie left Dan's house, Blaze became agitated. She began a ritual of pacing by the door until she exhausted herself. Only when Julie showed up would she settle down. When Dan would go out for a run, Blaze wanted no part of it.

Julie seemed to communicate with Blaze in a way that no one else could. Dan finally had to admit that he was no longer the master of his own dog. He asked Julie if she would like to have Blaze stay with her for a while.

"Oh Dan, are you sure? I know how much you love her," Julie said.

"Julie, if you want her—she has become a part of you."

And so, Blaze and Julie became inseparable. When Julie told Willow how it broke her heart when she had to leave her at the house every morning, Rita overheard the conversation.

"Land sakes, girl, bring her with you. Well, that is, if it's okay with you, Willow." She looked at Willow. "There are therapy dogs, right? Well this dog needs a therapy person to help her. Julie it sounds like you're it."

Willow agreed. "As long as she stays on the small porch off the kitchen while you're working, I can't see what it would hurt." So every morning Julie and Blaze walked together to the inn.

* * *

Julie had also kept busy untangling the legal mess of who she was and what her name should be. After much thought and many opinions from her Preston family as well as Katherine, she decided on the name Julie Lynn Preston. Katherine thought it sounded right, even though she sometimes slipped and called her Jennifer.

Katherine slowly began to come to terms with her late husband's past. She continued to have a hard time believing that Randolph had been responsible for murdering three people. But whatever had happened, the night that he found his daughter had changed his life. Katherine was sure of one thing—he had loved his daughter deeply. Katherine was in counseling for a short time, trying to figure out if he ever really loved her. She would never be certain. But she was grateful he had shared his daughter with her. Katherine looked forward to her frequent visits to Shady Creek to see Julie. Julie's family and friends always welcomed her, and she became close to Helen Barclay after they shared their feelings about the men each had loved and lost.

* * *

Helen had lived with a man who carried a lot of guilt with him for too many years. Now that the Prestons' granddaughter had finally been reunited with her family,

Helen prayed that Will was resting in his eternal life with a peace that he hadn't been able to find in his earthly life. She and Dan had visited Will's grave together shortly after Stanley Samuels' attack.

"Grams, I didn't understand before," Dan had explained. "But that day when I saw what that man did to Julie and Blaze, I couldn't think straight. I can't imagine what Granddad Will went through when he found his friends hacked up by some madman." Dan had stopped talking for a few minutes and stood staring at nothing, lost in his own thoughts. He finally finished, saying so softly, "I think I would have done anything to protect Julie and Blaze that day."

Helen had nodded. "I know how much your granddad loved his brother too. If things hadn't happened the way they did, Jimmy would probably have been blamed. I guess I can understand that part anyway."

Dan had drawn in a deep breath. "Just like everyone first blamed Larry."

That day seemed to be a breakthrough for Dan. He had gained an understanding of his grandfather's actions and was able to forgive his hero for the secret he'd held for so many years. Helen prayed that her grandson would now be able to go forward with his life.

She also knew he had fallen in love with Julie. And she knew it would not always be a perfect path for the two of them. She and Barbara talked about Dan and Julie building a life together. Both women hoped it would happen.

* * *

Richard Preston had also visited his old friend's grave again. He did not have the understanding that Dan had found. But now that his granddaughter was back in his life, he was not as bitter as he had been when he had first read Will's letters. If Will hadn't written those letters, no one would have known whether to believe Larry's crazy ghost story. He would never know why Randolph Kingman had to kill his daughter and two other people. And although he still had many questions, he knew in his heart that he would probably never find all the answers.

Today Richard and Barbara had just come from their lawyer's office. Richard's pocket held the deed for the house that Julie lived in. When she had finally settled all the legal issues with her name, the first thing he and Barbara had done was sign the house over to Julie Lynn Preston. The Prestons planned to give it to her on the first birthday they would get to celebrate with their granddaughter in more than twenty-three years. He knew Julie loved the house. He hoped someday Barbara and he might have a great-grandchild to play with in that house.

* * *

Barbara still had a sadness appear in her eyes once in awhile. But more often the sparkle shone through. Julie finally told her about HoHo's spontaneous rocking. At first Barbara was a bit jealous that she had never experienced the sensation of the little toy rocking under his own power or the aroma of the gingerbread that Julie told her about. And then she remembered the scene in the butterfly garden and knew that she had received her own special message, and just when she'd needed it most.

Now Barbara was working on getting Dan and Julie together, thinking that they were a perfect match. When she talked with Dan, she knew she was right. He was a patient man and was wise enough to know that Julie needed some time to find out who she really was. He would love her whether she was Julie, Jennifer, Jenny, or any other name she might decide on. After all, he had given her his best friend. He knew it was best for both of them.

* * *

Blaze didn't seem to mind the leash she had to wear now when she walked with Julie. She trusted Julie to let her know where she was allowed to go. So, as the weather turned nice and the greens of spring called to her, Julie thought they might try running again. Dan went with them the first couple of times, but neither woman nor dog wanted to run by the old bridge. When they went without Dan, they started slow and soon found the courage to go a little farther each day. They worked together to finally find the strength to go all the way to the bridge. And once they got there, they found no evil jumping out of the bushes to attack them.

Julie slowed her pace while they were on the bridge. Blaze glanced at her every so often, looking for reassurance. She stopped when they were in the center of the bridge and looked over the side where Larry Augustine had flung Stan's body. A small shiver ran down her spine. She was once again grateful to the friendly troll who had once lived under the bridge. She knew Dan had looked for Larry many times since he had become her unlikely hero. But no one in Shady Creek had seen anything of him since that day the previous fall. Julie looked down at Blaze and smiled. Blaze wagged her tail. They both turned and started their run back home.

Made in the USA
Charleston, SC
11 September 2011